TRIPPING FOR NUMBER 68

BOOK 1

THE SIN BIN SERIES

EDEN KNOX

DEDICATION

*For the hopeless romantics who also watch sports for the sports…
and also for the cute guys.*

*To my badass tattooed husband, who listens to me whine and isn't
scared to be eye candy for my fellow authors. You're the real MVP.
Love you.*

*To my friends and family who have spent decades now listening to
me be quirky and wandering the planet with my nose stuck in a
book. I love you all. But please do us both a favor and skip chapters
21, 22, 25, 27, 45, and 48. Yeah, definitely 27 and 48.*

CONTENT WARNING

Tripping For Number 68 is a steamy open door romance. This book does contain some topics that could be triggering for readers. Please be aware that this book contains descriptions of child illness, hospital settings, and treatment.

Passages also contain mild violence, profanity, and explicit sexual situations.

Reader discretion is advised.

CHAPTER 1

VERONICA

THERE ARE several things in life that are constants; taxes, death, sunrise and sunset. In my world, there was one other absolute; that Elliott "Eat Me" Moxley would be a gigantic dick in my presence. That's why it wasn't totally surprising when I experienced my early morning douchebaggery before I ever made it to the press offices of Theodore J. Price Arena. I definitely should have expected today to be topsy-turvy. My alarm didn't go off on time, I got stuck in rush hour traffic on my way to the arena, the parking garage entrance was closed for repairs, and worst of all my heel had just snapped off my boot while walking to the entrance and I hobbled the last 25 yards to the door. Frustrated, I try thinking on the bright side. It can always be worse, I think…until I ran squarely into Elliott Moxley's chest.

I bounce backwards, wobbling on the broken heel I swore I would glue back on when I got into the office; or maybe I would see if the skate shop could repair it for me. I spent far too much on this pair for them to die yet, and they were so comfortable! Desperately, I try to right myself before face planting on the concrete, only to lose my grip on the binders in my hand. Moxley's chest, a solid brick wall of muscle, gave me no help to stay upright as I land squarely on my knees against the cold concrete.

"Damnit," I curse under my breath, watching my pre-game notes scatter across the snow-dampened cement floor. Kneeling down to gather my belongings, I try not to pay attention to the towering man before me. One of his sneakers lifts slightly, and I watch him drop the toe onto a loose sheet of paper floating out of my reach. I let my gaze drift north; from the spotless shoes, up the endless stretch of denim, the curve of... okay, skipping that one. His white Ice Wolves tee is loosely tucked into his waistband, where it stretches over his pecs and shoulders. I look higher to make eye contact, only to see his cocky smirk, and for one of his green eyes to wink at me. He totally caught me looking.

"Mr. Moxley."

"Ms. Snow." My name on his lips is smooth, his deep timbre making it sound way more exotic and sensual than it really should in a workplace. "Dropped something," he says with a chuckle, and in reflex I roll my eyes. Elliott Moxley has been a thorn in my side since I started my internship with the press team. And after officially working here for three years, his demeanor still hasn't changed. Gathering sound bites and building posts for social media was my focus; producing the best optics possible for the team. The rest of the team had no problem sitting down with me but Moxley, he avoids me at all costs. He takes a knee in front of me, gathering up the documents farther away, and handing them over to me. Gritting my teeth, I stand back up with my belongings clutched to my chest.

"Yeah, I noticed," I mutter, gritting my teeth and remembering that I needed to at least act somewhat professional with him. "Thanks."

"Anytime. It's not every day I can get the Snow Queen to fall for me." He winks again, his cheeky grin growing more wolfish as I feel myself grimace. "Don't tell me cheesy lines like that actually work in real life? You can't actually be serious with that...that...," A disgusted sound erupts from my throat, which just makes him laugh.

"Aw, Ronni, you're going to hurt my feelings. Whatever will I do?"

"Don't you 'Ronni' me, Moxley. I still haven't forgiven you for standing me up last week for the promo shoot."

"I swapped with Kozlov! He worked out for you, didn't he?"

Something like a snort slips from me.. "Right. I specifically asked for you, and you sent me the rookie to do your dirty work. Besides, I needed face time and visuals, not audio spots. He had a black eye from the game the night before. He was hardly in any condition for a photo op."

"That was just the one time, though, I'm sure. I can't be that bad."

"You've rescheduled for every event I tapped you for. You also stood me up to go to the Sin Bin opening. Yes, you have a track record. No, I'm not impressed in the slightest." I wobbled on my broken shoe. He at least acknowledged that, as he stood up quicker and held out his large hand to steady me. I took it lightly and straightened myself, trying to ignore the unwelcome shiver from that small amount of contact.

"My bad. Next time? I promise I'll be there. I'll even bring you forgiveness cookies." His tone told me he wasn't sorry.

"Whatever. Just do what I ask of you, and quit trying to do my job for me." Laying a shaky palm across my papers, I turn on my heel, feeling my ponytail swing behind me. "Also, it will take a lot more than some cookies to get in my good graces. Try harder."

I hurry my pace down the hall, while carefully trying to keep my balance on my uneven heels. The unmitigated gall of that man! He struts around this arena as if he owned the place! Conceited, smug, he flashes that smile and gets whatever he wants!

He probably isn't a totally horrible person, and I'm just being mean about it. The kids love him at events because he knows how to talk to them at their level. As the captain of the Ice Wolves, it's been said that he has amazing skills on ice, his game strategy can't be beat, and his puck handling led to a strong winning streak last season. His players respect him on ice and off, and they work together like a well-oiled machine. He had some issues with on-ice fighting, but that adds to his fan appeal. This season is just starting, but the fans agree that if he can keep his nose clean and his focus on the game, there could be a playoff run in their future.

Okay, he's a beautiful human and a fantastic hockey player; however, his personality and his ability to follow my instructions is subpar at best. He has a reputation for being a "bad boy," and seen in clubs and with several high profile, high drama models that made him go viral before. His latest girlfriend dropped a massive article in the tabloids about their relationship, complete with pictures and screenshots. The photo explosion during the playoffs didn't help matters. Sure, the female fan base enjoyed seeing all sides of him, and the ticket and merch sales definitely backed that up. But the irresponsible, class clown pranking his teammates during interviews? The no-show events that left me scrambling? That side of Elliot Moxley made my job ten times harder than it needed to be, but it kept me gainfully employed. Even his penalty minutes were out of control, even if they were justified.

I push open the door to the public relations office and hobble to my cubicle. Thanks to freaking God or some other deity that I kept an extra pair of shoes at my desk. I sigh as I slip on the black ballet flats, regretting the choices I'd made until this point of the day.

"Freaking egotistical, useless, waste of space, ugh!" I kick my broken boot under my desk with a curse before turning my attention to my computer's loading screen and the haphazard stack of papers I had gathered off the floor. My prep time for the day was non-existent, and now I have to reprint my work and put the folders back together. I would lay the blame for that squarely at his stupid feet. Running into Moxley, literally and figuratively, set my whole schedule off for the day.

"Problems, Ronni?" Jessica peers around the corner at me, sipping her coffee from her paper cup while handing me another one. She has been my sister-in-arms, my best friend since I started with the Ice Wolves. Her focus this season was on the Ice Wolves Foundation, the charity wing attached to the team, which puts us on the same projects occasionally. I took the proffered cup, and smiled gratefully for the coffee, before frowning a bit at the recollection.

"Oh, you know, just another lovely run-in with my favorite. I swear, sometimes I hope he gets traded so I can stop dealing with him and his crap." I took a sip of the coffee and sighed in happiness. "Plus, those were my favorite boots, I'm so bummed!"

"It could be so much worse, though. Remember the mess we had to go through when the goalies had that yacht party in Miami? That took forever to fix! At least Moxley is simple, even if he's consistent." Her shoulders shrug, and she sips from her own cup. "A single puck bunny making negative press because he dumped her is way easier than a dozen drunken bunnies on a boat."

I scrunch my face as I remember the fallout from that particular event. "Yeah, you're right. It's just the consistency of it all that drives me crazy." Movement catches my attention behind her, and a smile spreads on my face "Hey, what do we have on the docket today, Michael?"

Michaeal Rockford walks toward my desk and carefully hands me a thick envelope. I glance at it, noting the inter office directions—the documents traveled from the commissioner's office to Michael, specifically. My heart rate jumps at the implication. Messages from the head office could go either way.

"Go ahead, Ronni, open it." His eyes are wide with excitement, and he bounces on the heels of his worn out loafers, his breathing growing a little wheezy. I worry, for about the thousandth time since I'd met him, that he was going to have a medical event.

"I take it you know what's in here already, and I'm not going to ugly cry?"

"I wouldn't intentionally make you cry, you're my favorite PR specialist."

Unraveling the string, I pull out the folder, slowly taking in the contents. Before me, in a confidential memo, lay the workings of what the head office wants from the resident bad boy. He has until the end of the season to straighten up or he's on the chopping block. He's a liability to the image of the team. I read through the recommendations, photo ops and charity events recommended to clean up his image, community outreach opportunities, and at the very bottom of the last page, a recommendation for a handler...followed by my name.

"Michael, no. No! Absolutely not. Why me?" "Ronni, you're the best we have for this. If anyone can fix it for him, you can. Plus, it could lead to big things for you here. If you make this happen, there could be a massive promotion in the works."

"Like how massive are we talking? This could be a ton of extra work besides my current projects." I glance at the list again. "I see at least 3 more major events here, plus the Foundation's charity ball is in a few months. I'll be lucky if you see me doing anything else for the rest of the season besides babysitting him."

"Like you could be fast tracked to my executive assistant, and intended to replace me when I retire in five years. That's kind of massive." My jaw dropped.

This is really enormous. This could be career changing!

"I can take some of your extra side projects off your hands, but this is your focus."

I look back down at the folder and wish that the ground had actually swallowed me whole before I came to work today. Suffocating on earth would be better than realizing that for the next six months, or longer, I would be in close contact with Elliot Freaking Moxley on a nearly daily basis. "If it's what I have to do," I reply. I can do this. I've dealt with worse, I think. Besides, what's the worst that could happen while trying to reform the current bad boy of the Ice Wolves?

CHAPTER 2

ELLIOT

I FREAKING LOVE MY JOB. I know everyone says that, but I do. I mean, how many people can actually say that they get to play their favorite game, live out their childhood dreams, and get paid to do it? Signing on with the Ice Wolves after my senior year of college was a legitimate dream come true and even though there had been some hurdles, I regret nothing. Even the occasional run-in with the media didn't dull the shine.

Sure, I was walking on some thin ice with Coach right now. A few perfect storms last year put me in a questionable public relations state. I hoped the off-season would have dulled the roar. I wasn't exactly an altar boy and had the occasional PR incident. But it didn't mean I was totally bad, right?

There were rumblings last season that I spent too much time at clubs. Then there was the noise about the visible tattoos. But come on, how long could news outlets really cling to the fact that my latest ex had released pics of my junk on social media, which led to other exes coming out of the woodwork to corroborate? It wasn't my choice or my fault directly. They're still going on about it six months later, though, and I know the owners are still hot, and not in a good way. That means I have to do the one thing I don't really like.

Groveling.

Coach said I have until the end of the season or he's going to recommend me for a trade. I get it, really.

The organization always comes first, and they can't damage their reputation just to save me. I can do this, though, I know I can fix this. I'm only a few years into what could be the next 15 years of my life, if I'm lucky. It's rare a player stays with one team for a duration like that, but I want to try. I want to stay, set up roots and call this place my home. The lifespan of a professional hockey player is roughly the equivalent of a small house pet. The average player may get a handful of seasons. Clearing a decade is phenomenal. At any moment I could face a career-ending injury and never see ice time again. If I make it to the ripe old age of 30 without becoming a peewee coach in some rundown rink somewhere, then I will consider myself lucky.

I should have known better than to trust myself around Lacey. The guys told me she was a puck bunny, but I didn't listen. She was gorgeous, and she treated me like the rockstar I thought I was, until I told her I needed to focus on my career instead of going to random parties. I thought she understood and that it could be amicable until our private texts and pics hit the internet. All hell broke loose after that. Team ownership wasn't happy about the partying and the optics from that, and they put their foot down. She didn't appreciate being passed over, and boy, did she let me see it. Hell has no fury or something like that. Less than a week into playoffs last spring, and she dropped all of our private texts and pictures to the highest bidder. I spent three weeks juggling the hardest games of my season and the fallout from that. On top of the twenty-thousand dollars she made, her name was also plastered everywhere, just like she always wanted. I lost our spot in the playoffs and was left with just a string of viral posts and soundbites asking if my off-ice issues translated into my issues on-ice. I'll never forget or forgive myself for that. The failure fell completely on my shoulders as the team captain.

The off-season gave me lots of time to reflect, and visualize how my career and history could pan out from here. I have a list in my back pocket to run by Coach and see if I can redeem myself with some publicity events. I will gladly put myself at the mercy of our PR team; they knew what would help fix this. Although, I feel like it would work better for all parties involved if I worked with anyone other than Miss Veronica Snow.

She insists I call her Veronica. I've heard her telling Jonesy at an event once that only friends get to call her Ronni. He got to call her Ronni, naturally. Hell, even the team assistants and the arena janitorial team call her Ronni. I don't know what I did to be excluded from that, but my mama taught me to be respectful so I will "Miss Veronica Snow" her until she changes her mind.

There was something about her that just got under my skin, and I wonder if she felt a fraction of that about me as well. That fiery personality, her inability to relax and take things in stride, the way she won't just let me "aw, shucks" my way out of anything, it pushes me harder to prove her wrong about me. She treats me like I'm any other anonymous jock on the team and no matter how much I try to say I don't care, I do. I can't help it. I want her to like me. No. I need her to like me, and I still can't grasp why that's so damn important.

On top of that, she has this nerdy-hot thing going on; messy buns held up with pens, prim little outfits with cardigans. That's not my usual type, but I can't deny that watching her on her knees a second ago did something to me. I know, I know, don't shit where you eat, and don't dip your quill in the company's ink, I've heard all the phrases before. But still.

There's something about watching her cheeks turn pink when things aren't to her standard that is just freaking adorable. And knowing I'm the one that made her blush? It's a high like no other.

"Get your shit together, Mox," I grumble before pushing open the doors to the team locker room. I breathe in deeply, allowing the box breath technique to calm me. Four seconds in, four seconds out, while looking across the open space, the wall of black and blue jerseys hanging uniformly in each locker cubicle. This is my home, this is where I am centered.

Walking over to my locker, I run my fingertips over the large black "68" embroidered on the back of my sky blue Ice Wolves jersey. This is what I have dreamed of doing since I could lace up skates by myself. I hope to live up to the history behind this jersey. There have been a long line of superstars that have carried this number to great heights, and I hope to fulfill that in my career.

"Moxley, get your ass in here!" Coach's voice carries across the room and jolts me back to the present. Rolling the stiff muscles in my neck, I breathe and slowly exhale. He sounds royally pissed, and I know I won't look forward to this at all. With one last glance at my number, I walk toward his office.

"You wanted to see me, Coach," I say, hoping to sound calm while crossing the threshold into his office. I drop into a seat and will my heart to stop racing. *It's going to be fine*, I think to myself; he couldn't cut me with the C on my sweater, but he can certainly make life complicated for me. Or, at least, that's what I told myself. He wouldn't actually trade me... right?

Coach didn't even look up at my voice. He just kept typing away at his computer, pounding hard enough that I could hear the plastic groaning under his heavy hands. Yeah, this won't be good. He leaves me to sit there wordlessly, with only the abuse of his keyboard breaking up the silence. This didn't bode well at all.

"Moxley, what did I tell you boys before we started the pre-season? What did I expect from the team, and most importantly, you?"

I take a fortifying breath and recite his speech from the first day of camps. "You want us to focus on the ice and keep our noses clean. Stay out of trouble, both on ice and off, sir." I remember that speech like it was yesterday. "I have really worked hard to improve what gets printed about me, I swear. I cut out the parties, and I've put in extra rink time. I put-"

He cut me off with an impatient wave of his thick hand. "I know, I know, Mox. But the front office wants to see something more public from you. They feel like a few meet and greet type events may help clear up some misunderstandings from your previous relationship."

I curse under my breath. My "previous relationship," I know just what he means. I regret ever laying eyes on Lacey and thinking I could ever avoid this exact situation. I wasn't above this. I knew she wanted publicity and knew in my gut that I'd get burned by her. I know now that anyone who carries a selfie stick in their purse is not looking to get to know you, just what your face can do for their follower count.

"What does the head office propose that I do about this?"

"They have a plan, but it's going to be a lot of hard work for you. There's going to be a series of community events that the PR office needs warm bodies for, so expect to hear from Ronni soon. You are her main go-to. Jess may also use you for Foundation projects, but not as much. I don't care what else you have going on, you're doing this first. Do I make myself clear?"

"Crystal, Coach." I feel some of the tension ease out of my shoulders. This wasn't "The Talk" that I thought it would be, but I didn't totally dodge that bullet, either. Ronni–I mean, Veronica—wouldn't be going to make it easy on me, and I'm pretty sure she hated my guts. However, what head office ever says is gospel, so I didn't have room to argue with them. I just needed to nod my head and move on.

With a firm nod of my head, I promise to do whatever he needed me to do for the team; that was easy. I will keep my nose clean, I would do everything they asked of me, and spend countless hours signing autographs and taking pictures, every chance I could get. This means far too much for me to screw it up.

Walking out of his office with a renewed sense of purpose, I swore on my prized autographed Mario Lemieux jersey that I would never, ever let a woman interfere with my career again.

CHAPTER 3

VERONICA

I SIT down at my desk, looking at my still unanswered emails from Elliot "I don't have a computer" Moxley. I grit my teeth and tried not to growl in frustration. It's been two weeks since Michael gave me my new assignment. Thirteen days since I emailed Elliot himself. The next day I sent one to the "assistant to the assistant of his agent" looking for his latest schedule of events because I had nothing from the man himself. It's also been 10 days since I got his cell number from Alexandr Kozlov. I even had Michael drop a line down through the chain that he needed to get up here, thinking that his title would make something happen. Granted, there were two back-to-back travel games in the middle there, but the whole team has been back for a full week and still I heard nothing.

"Jess, what does a girl have to do to get a call back around this place?" I toss a blue rubber stress ball across the cubicle divider. I hear her giggle on the other side, before the ball comes back across the wall toward me. "I'm serious though, it's been forever and I've gotten nothing!"

"The team has barely been home in what, a couple weeks now? I'm running out of stored drafts to post, it's getting dire over here." Jess's chair rolls over so she could peek around the corner of my cubicle. "At this rate, I'll need to film the therapists and equipment managers for material."

"I know, it's been a while. It still didn't stop any of them from clubbing and posting their own media. I mean, Moxley had time to do a freaking keg stand between two road games, but not answer a damn email. How do I know, you ask? I found it while looking for a response from him about setting up a meeting. And even if he gets back to me now, I have to go into the PR meeting in 15 minutes and say I've had zero contact with the only major project to my name. It's ridiculous!"

"Well, it got a lot of views, and talk of a new endorsement opportunity with a local brewery. They emailed for meet and greet opportunities." Jess ducked the ball I lob back at her again. "Just call it the way it is, Ronni! Say that you haven't had a face-to-face meeting yet, but it's in the works, and then give your list of planned events for him."

"I know, and it's not that I have accomplished nothing in the last week or so, it's just that I have zero confirmation that his schedule will allow for any of it. His agent was apparently on vacation the last two weeks." I pick up my coffee cup, which was now nearly empty and cold. "This isn't fair!" I whine as I drop my forehead across my folded arms, feeling my ponytail flare out around my head. "I can't believe I'm about to say this, but all I want is proof of life from that royal pain in my butt and a candy bar. A fresh coffee would be nice too. I don't think I'm asking for the freaking moon here. I just want cooperation from the freaking man."

"I can run out for the coffee and maybe snag candy bar if you want, but I'm here. I'm assuming you're talking about me." My breath freezes in my lungs at the deeper voice coming from behind me. Slowly, I lift my head off my desk, before turning to look at the mystery speaker.

"Um, hi." There he is, actually here, leaning against my

cubicle wall. Panic left me blinking up at him. "Sorry, I didn't mean for that to sound like it did. You're just a really hard guy to get in touch with."

"Does it help that I have a good excuse, or maybe a few good excuses?" His boyish grin is disarming, as always, but I can't let myself forget he had thrown me so far off the schedule that my frustration is justified.

"Not particularly. I have to cram twice as many events into half the time now if we're going to save your reputation. We've lost weeks of planning. Do you have free time to meet up soon? Tomorrow, maybe? I really need to iron out details so we can get you onto the event schedule, publicize everything, you know," I pause trying to choose my words carefully, "the things I need to do my job effectively for you."

Pulling his phone out, and without even flipping through the notifications on his lock screen, he glances at his calendar. "I have an early practice in the morning but I should be able to meet up after that around 10."

I block off time on my calendar, and nod. "That looks great, let's meet next door then, so you don't have to go super far after practice. If you're going to be late, drop me a text or something, okay?"

"Will do. See you tomorrow, Snow Queen!"

He turns to leave before he can see my eye roll, but it feels satisfying anyway. I reach for my coffee and prepare to take a calming sip, before grimacing at the lukewarm liquid. Turning toward Jess's cubicle, as expected, her head is peeking over the top of the wall, her usual impish grin in place.

"You couldn't have said something? Some friend you are!"

"It looked like you two had it well under control, you didn't need me," she laughs. "Seriously, though, I don't think he had a problem with anything you said." I shoot her an incredulous look. "You didn't see his face beforehand, I think he enjoys irritating you."

"That has to be one of the dumbest things I've ever heard, he liked me talking about him like that?

That's like saying that boys in school like you because they tug on your pigtails, get out of here with that mess."

"Girl, you didn't see him coming up. He knew what you were talking about and had a hard time trying not to laugh the whole time! He was in on it!"

"How long was he in here," I screech, trying to school my features. My eyes go wide in shocked mortification. "Crap, I'm going to get fired. I'm going to get removed from the arena for talking smack about the captain. I'm just going to pack my things now."

"Ronni, it's not that serious. He heard, but he was also laughing the whole time. Relax. Just buckle down and get his schedule figured out so you can take over the team!"

I know she's speaking the truth, but it just feels like everything is stacked against me. "I'll try. Hey, I'll see you in the meeting, I'm stopping out front at The Den for more coffee first."

She waves her goodbye to me, and I head out toward the front of the arena so I can hit my favorite coffee joint in the pavilion outside the arena. Pulling open their app while I walk down the empty hallway, I start my order to save some time, only to—

"Shit!" A male voice curses as I struggle to stay upright, and I gasp as hot liquid soaks through my shirt.

"Damnit!" I shriek at about the same time, watching my phone clatter to the floor, splashing into a puddle of coffee. "I'm so sorry, I didn't—Moxley?"

Standing before me, his previously white t-shirt now mottled with splotches of coffee and—is that whipped cream on his shoulder? Yes, that was definitely whipped cream melting on his shoulder, and sliding down his biceps, to drip off of his elbow. Elliot Moxley was most definitely wearing a whole cup of coffee.

"Oh no, are you okay?" He moves quickly, kneeling to pick up my phone and dry it off on a portion of his t-shirt that somehow missed the shower of coffee. "Here, I think it survived the fall. Did it get on you?"

"Mine? What about you?" I wave a hand in his general direction. "That shirt will never recover either."

"It's nothing, I keep a couple changes down in the locker room." His gaze darted around, looking everywhere but at me. "Um, I can see if the fan shop has anyone in it to get you a replacement shirt. But you might want to head somewhere else, and soon, if you don't want anyone to see you out here like this."

I look down in horror at the grave state of my shirt. The light blue shirt had gone nearly translucent and I could definitely see my bra through it. Mortification. I could feel panic building in my chest, my harsh breaths, feeling wheezy, and I looked around for somewhere, anywhere, I could go to take care of this. Or hide. Hiding sounds optimal.

"Crap crap crap I have a meeting with the PR department in like, 15 minutes! I'm never getting there now!" I spun on my heel, walking quickly toward my cubicle. If I'm lucky, I still had a spare promotional t-shirt or something at my desk and I could at least salvage the top half of my attire beforehand.

"Wait, Ronni— I mean Veronica— hold up!" I hear him behind me, his longer strides eating up the space between us. "Hey, wait, come in here." I feel his hand warm on my back, guiding me toward one of the women's rooms. Before I can say anything, he reaches for the towel dispenser and then wets a handful down. "Go in and try to get the worst of it off. There's not a lot worse than drying drinks. I'll be right back. Okay? Don't go anywhere."

I lock the stall door behind me, lean against the wall, and take a deep breath. What a mess, I think, as I peeled the wet fabric away from me. I throw the wet shirt across the top of the door, and dabbed away at the coffee splotches on my skin. My bra is damp, but not super horrible. I wipe at it with a handful of towels, and hoped for the best. Looking down at my phone, I swipe at the screen to clear up the sticky residue, and then drop a text at least to Jess and let her know I'm running a few minutes behind.

Deep breaths, Ronni, it will be okay.

My phone buzzes in my hand and I look down to see two texts that arrived almost at the same time.

Jess: No problem, I'll let them know you're on the way in a few!

Moxley: Hey, don't panic. Shop was closed but I have something in my locker that may work. I'll be right back. Promise.

I released a relieved breath, feeling a little better about the situation knowing that Jess is communicating with the team, and she would get things taken care of starting the meeting. Knowing that I'm stuck in a public bathroom without a proper shirt on, waiting on the man who has been dodging me for two weeks to come back with a clean shirt? That made me more nervous.

Patience was never one of my virtues and here I was, waiting. My thoughts spiraled. He wouldn't leave me here like this, right? I tap out another text to Jess, giving her the gory details of what went down on my way to get coffee, and hit send. Then, I grit my teeth and wait.

"Okay, I'm coming in. I hope this doesn't fit too horribly, it was all I had in my locker that wasn't sweaty." His voice boomed off the walls as I hear him come closer. "Here, take this," his disembodied voice says as a hand with a wadded cloth came across the door, "and I'll take this one and try to rinse it out. The trainer I passed said to get cold water so it wouldn't set." My wet shirt disappeared while he talked. I grabbed what he delivered and feel my panic bubble as I look at his navy game day jersey.

"Your game jersey? You need this for tomorrow night, I can't take this!"

"Technically it's my alternate jersey that we aren't wearing tomorrow, and I also know that you're going to get it back to me in time because you're anal-retentive like that. Also, if it bothers you that much, I can get this shirt down in the trainer laundry in less than five minutes and we can swap this evening after your meeting. Your call."

A shirt is a shirt, I tell myself as I pull the heavy material over my head. *But it's not just wearing a shirt when it's a player's jersey,* a small voice in the back of my head argued back. Wearing one of the mass produced out of the fan shop was one thing; wearing their own was on par with wearing your boyfriend's letterman jacket in high school.

"Desperate times," I mutter to myself as I open the door and stare at Elliot Moxley, hunched over a sink, carefully washing my shirt out, his forehead furrowed in concentration. He clearly changed shirts while downstairs, but the crumples made me wonder if it had been balled up in the bottom of his locker. "This thing is massive, but it works. The important bits are covered and professional. Thanks," I say as I smoothed out the logo patch, the hemline falling mid-thigh on my jeans.

"Yeah, sorry about that, they're always like two sizes too big to fit over…," his words trail off as he glances up from the mirror, frozen. "Yeah, I think that will work just fine. It's perfect." His voice a little hoarse compared to normal. With a small cough to clear his throat, he turned to stare down at my sodden shirt again.

"Thank you, I mean it. You didn't have to run all the way to the locker room to get me a shirt."

"No, I did. It's the least I could do after spilling your coffee on you."

I tilt my head in confusion. "My coffee? I hadn't ordered yet, what are you talking about?"

"I went to get you coffee. Thankfully Marie knows who you are and what you always order. You said you needed it so… yeah. And now here we are. Although you may want to head to your meeting before you're late. I'll get a replacement at your desk in a few, and I'll get this down in the laundry." He didn't look up once while carefully wringing out the water from the cloth in his hands.

"Thanks, Moxley. Um, I'll text you when I'm done." I start to walk out, my ballet flats tapping softly on the concrete.

"Hey, Snow Queen?" He calls from behind me.

I pause, glancing back to look at him, his large hands resting on the lip of the sink, his head bowed over my shirt. Slowly, he turned to face me, his grin making that dimple pop. His eyes flashed with that mischievous look that I was used to seeing on the Jumbotron before face off.

"Maybe you should keep it. My number looks better on you than it does on me."

I snorted and rolled my eyes at him, ignoring his chuckle echoing off the walls in my wake.

CHAPTER 4

VERONICA

I SIT at the cafe table just outside the arena the next morning, watching for Moxley to come through the door for our meeting. He was, much to my irritation, late. Again. Not even a little late; I'd been here for half an hour at this point waiting for him to show up for a meeting I didn't even want to have. This was his idea, and he couldn't even have the common decency to show up? I scowl at my laptop screen as I furiously type out a series of social media posts to schedule for the weekend and then settle back with my cooling latte. My phone dings just as I decide to give up, and the door swinging wide as Elliot barrels in, as if the hounds of hell followed him.

I startle at the disruption, frowning. He flops into the chair beside me, an impish grin on his face as he shoots a look toward the barista and winks. From her answering smile and the way she prepares a drink, apparently he is a regular too. Of course he gets whatever he wants without a word. Freaking playboy.

Looking him over, the shower-damp hair catching the morning sun coming through the window, wearing the "Property of the Ice Wolves" t-shirt that we just dropped into the team shop a couple weeks ago, and the dark blue jeans clinging to his thighs, and the skater shoes I recognized from previous events, I feel my annoyance simmering. Maybe practice ran late, but he still put himself together for being out.

"You're late." My words are clipped, and I don't even make eye contact with him as I finish what I was working on. I couldn't be bothered with professional niceties at the moment, and I didn't care how it made me look. "I have other things to do today besides loiter around here waiting on you to grace me with your presence."

"I know, I know, sorry. Did you know there was a field trip to the arena? I walked right into the herd of kids, so I did the nice thing and stopped for pictures and autographs. Sorry about that, I should've emailed or something. Can I get you a refill? I think I owe you a coffee. Or a muffin. Or both. Just not cookies, I remember you said no cookies before."

"I didn't say no cookies, I said you owe me a hell of a lot more than cookies for the stress you put me under, Mr. Moxley. There's a difference." I slide my mouse to open up my calendar app. "We have a lot of work to do and not a lot of time to do it. Are you prepared for all of this?"

He nods his head, his longer blond hair swirling around in the late morning light. "I am, I know that I need this a lot. I don't want to leave the team, I have…plans. I need to stay here." I note the delay in his response, feeling like he's hiding something. I just can't tell what.

"Fine, then let's get started," I say while turning my laptop around so he can see what I was working with. "This is the current calendar of events I've built for you; it's not complete, but it gives us a place to start. I have the game and travel schedule on board already. I'm going to need a copy of your workout schedule so I can work around that, too. Also, any new dates or pre-confirmed events from your agent, I'll need to add it into mine as well. I tried to ask, but he's out of town."

"No problem, my workout schedule is easy. On regular practice days I'm in and out of the gym by 7am, skate is done by noon. You tell me where you want me, and you've got it." He grins, flashing me bright teeth and a dimple in his right cheek. I raise an eyebrow in disbelief.

"That's it? That's all your normal day consists of is gym time and a morning skate? No wonder you have so much time to blow me off and get into trouble," I mutter under my breath, furiously typing an email to his agent and Elliot's team email.

"I don't honestly try to get in trouble; I just want to play hockey and do well for the team."

I jolt; I didn't think he heard me, and it surprised me he felt like that. Pausing in my typing, I glance over my screen. His forehead was creased, and that grin had fallen into a straight line, his pulse visible in his clenched jaw.

"Don't take it so hard; some chicks dig the bad boys." I smile reassuringly, lightening the heavy mood around us.

"You say that like you know from experience."

I snort. "Hardly. They're far more work than I care to have. If I wanted a relationship that was built on chaos and unruly behavior, I'd get myself a puppy."

His phone buzzed from the tabletop, and a quick glance at the screen showed a girl's name. I groan inwardly. Of course he has a girl as his escape route from this meeting. It continued to ring, and I studied Elliot's face, his eyes never wavering from me.

"Are…you going to answer that?" I ask, nodding toward the phone dancing precariously close to the edge of the table. He glances down at it, shifting it closer to the center of the table with a finger, then stares right back at me.

"Nope. This is a work meeting, and I'm focusing on work. You know, and I know, that I need to make this season the best I've ever had. I don't need the distractions." The phone fell silent for a moment, and then promptly buzzed again, with a text notification and another girl's name. I noticed he didn't look down at it.

"Well then, let's move forward with..." I sigh, halting my words as the buzzing started again with a completely different girl's name on his screen. I raise my eyebrow and motion toward it again. "How about you take five and sort out your fan club, okay?"

He looked down, jolting. "I need to take this one, though. I'm sorry, I'll be right back." He unfolds himself from the chair, answering as he steps away. "Hey, Princess Buttercup..."

His words fade into nothing as he worked his way toward the door. I grit my teeth as I once again realize I've been blown off with this project. Again. I muttered under my breath as I built the schedule for our future events without him. His agent answers back while he's gone with a few signing events, and a couple Make-A-Wish appointments, so I add those into the schedule as I went.

I look up to see if he was coming back, just in time to watch him pass a handful of fans, dropping signatures with his phone still in the crook of his neck. He smiles pleasantly at them as he slowly returned to the table.

"Okay, be a good girl and I'll see you later, right? Love you, Princess." He hangs up the call and then slides a large thumb over the airplane mode icon. "Sorry about that, I can't let her go to voicemail."

"It's fine, whatever," I wave it off. "Your agent gave me your upcoming events. It may be tight but I think we can work with that. I have some school groups coming into the arena in a couple weeks that I don't have players attached to yet, and there's the foundation ball in April that I'll definitely need you for, but that's months away."

He nodded his head in agreement and pulls up his calendar on the app. "Did Ryan send you the hospital visits? Those are non-negotiable, I have to go to those events."

I poured over the list I received, and frowned. "The only visit I see is the Make-A-Wish, but that's at the arena, not the hospital. What dates are you locked down, so I can adjust?" My phone pings with an alert, and I see that he's shared his calendar with me. I opened the calendar, my eyes widening. "Every other week? That's a large amount of time!"

"I know. But I can't miss these. Everything has to adjust around those."

I balk at the overlapping dates. Events that would be huge for his improved optics, now completely unavailable because of this. I grit my teeth and take a breath.

"It will be a huge ordeal. I mean, there's at least five events that would help your cause with the team that you can't do because of these…unsanctioned events? I mean, it's your party, Moxley, but you might need to reconsider."

He glances at the screen again and then shakes his head violently. "No. Absolutely not. It's a hard pass."

"Fine," I sighed. "So, the first event I should use you for would be next week at the local school pep rally event. Thursday night before the game, there's a meet and greet with students, locker room tours, then ice time with them, before game prep. Cool?"

"Yeah," he replies, typing into his phone.

"So, there's also the Foundation Ball to consider. Jess is putting together some kind of bachelor auction to raise funds, are you willing to play along?"

"Sure, anything that would help. I can even sign a few things, maybe donate some of my game gear if it will help."

My eyes shoot up from my laptop in surprise. "That will help. Get me a list of items that you're open to donating and I'll get it in front of her."

In what seems like no time, an alarm goes off on his phone.

"Great. So, are we done? I kind of need to bounce."

"You seriously just got here!"

"I know, but I have this appointment I need to get to, and I thought we were mostly done. Shoot me the schedule when you get it ironed out, okay? Thanks, Snow Queen!"

I stare after him in disbelief, feeling my anger flare again. He's not taking this seriously in the slightest! It's like high school and doing school projects for the jocks all over again. If I get fired because of him, I will be so pissed.

CHAPTER 5

I TOOK serious risks coming here, but I couldn't leave her alone. My girl is the reason I do all of this. She's why I show up at clubs to drum up business for friends, why I've pushed for bonuses and visibility, and she's the only reason I'm trying so damn hard to save my contract before it disappears into thin air before me.

Gabby was never part of my plan. She's not even mine; she's my niece, my little sister Sami's kid, officially. When things got rough and the expenses were too much for her, I did what I always did as Sami's big brother; I picked up the pieces and held everything together. As a hotshot hockey superstar making obscene amounts of money from endorsements and playing a sport as a job, it's the least I could do to help. So here I was, serial bachelor and financial caretaker to my sister and niece. Not that anyone else knew that. My publicist, my agent, anyone who is involved in my life and had to know, has been sworn to secrecy. It's more for her well-being than anything. Her safety could be compromised if someone wanted to use her to get to me. So here I am, sneaking in the hospital to see my niece, the child I've taken care of for the last year, and no one is the wiser.

"Uncle El!" Her voice is soft, weaker than the excitement she tries to exude. Today must have been a rough day.

"Hey, Princess Buttercup, how are you feeling?" I slide into the hard plastic chair and take in her pale face, the dark circles under her eyes.

She grimaces a little, which tells me everything. I pick up her small hand and run my thumb along her knuckles, careful not to get too close to the IV taped to her wrist. Treatment week is always hard on her, but this one seemed to be harder than before.

This has, unfortunately, been part of the process. The doctor appointments, the hospital visits, the nanny and tutor to do her schooling anywhere, it is all a part of our new normal. She has taken everything in stride, considering how scary the whole situation is. We're making it through, though, one day at a time.

"Where's your ma, I thought she'd be up here with you?"

"She went down for a coffee, but said she'd be back in a few minutes. Do you have time to read with me, Uncle El?"

"As you wish," I respond with a smile. No matter what went on with her treatments, reading was always our hobby together. When I played away games, we would FaceTime and read together as well. It helped keep her mind off of the pain usually. "Where should we start this time? We could pick up Princess Bride again or," I pause for dramatic effect, "we could see what I picked up from the bookstore on the way over."

"Gimme!" The energy she put in that one word as she shot upright to reach for me was impressive.

I hand her the paper bag with a chuckle, watching her tear into the packaging with joy. She'll be exhausted later, but seeing her act like a normal kid for a moment makes my heart lurch in my chest. She should worry about her grades, friends, maybe trying to figure out what sport to play.

Instead, she's sitting here learning words far above what her 7-year-old maturity level should know.

A small selfish part of myself was angry that she wouldn't get to experience what the other kids did, including my teammates' kids. No free skates with us pre-game, she can't risk the fall. She can't come with me to team events in case someone exposes her to an illness, or even worse, become a target because of my reputation…guilt hits me for my carelessness early in my career. She could have had it so much better if I had made better steps, wiser choices.

"Yes, new manga! You're the best, Uncle El!" Holding the paperback aloft in her bruised and pale hands, her smile brightening her face, I can't help but grin back. Her excitement is palpable. "I've heard of this series! It's almost impossible to find!"

"I have my ways." I reach into the bag and pull out a second copy. "I even got myself a copy so we can buddy read it while I'm on the road. We can FaceTime it."

I can see her move to say something, but movement distracts her at the door. Her mom is leaning against the doorway smiling at us. I smile back, moving to get up.

"I'm going to go talk to your ma, okay? Don't read too far ahead of me, remember your uncle is just a dumb jock."

"I'll be fine, Uncle El."

I unfold from the tiny chair and walk out into the hallway.

"Hey El." My sister's voice was gravelly and soft, tired sounding. I really looked at her, the dark circles under her eyes more prominent than they have been.

Her oversized flannel hung limply over her wrinkled band tee, and I wonder if she had gone home at all since yesterday. Her lean against the rail on the wall looks casual on the surface, but the white-knuckle grip contradicted with her relaxed form.

She was tense, nervous, and her anxiety made my heart race.

"What's the story, Morning Glory? Do you have an update from the doctors? What's going on?"

She pauses, looking up at me. Flashbacks hit me, times in our childhood when she had the same conflicted look; she had backed her car into the neighbor's fence when she wasn't supposed to be driving yet, or the time she had failed a required course for her degree and had to tell Mom about it. More recently, when she found out she was pregnant with Gabby and then when she found out Gabby was sick, the same unsure expression was impossible for her to mask.

"The doctors want us to move forward with the bone marrow transplant. They think it is her best option at this point if we can find a match."

I nod, recalling the previous meetings we'd had with her care team in the last month. They weren't wrong; it had a high probability of working but it required testing anyone with a genetic link to Gabby, including her father.

"But this requires talking to her dad and his family." There it was. The elephant in the room, the Beetlejuice level specter in our family. My heart cracked at the pained expression in her face but it had to be exposed. We've never asked his name out loud since the day she found out she was pregnant and refused to tell us anything, and for good reason. Anyone willing to just abandon their pregnant girlfriend and stay out of contact for the better part of a decade is not worth our time or voice, whoever he might have been. Sami's decision to keep it secret is her choice. "Where is he now, do you know?"

She nods her head slowly. "I know where he is, but I don't have his current contact information. I could get it, though."

"You know what you need to do, Sami, and I have your back no matter what. But if his side has the donor…," I leave the statement hanging, she knows what I mean.

"I know. In the meantime, there's a shot at a donor match coming from within the network, but there are better odds of a familial match."

"We'll do what we need to do. Gabby always comes first." I hold my arms open to my little sister, enveloping her smaller frame in my large arms. "Did you eat tonight?" I sigh when she shook her head no. "Come on, let me feed you. And then I can tell you all about what I've gotten up to with my new professional babysitter."

"Elliot, please be nice to that poor woman. I know you don't like having to answer to anyone but maybe you need to let her get you situated for once."

"What are you talking about? I'm on my best behavior with her!"

Sami's snort tells me everything I need to know. She knows me better than I know myself sometimes, so I can't hide anything from her. I throw her an innocent shrug, refusing to admit that I enjoy antagonizing the shit out of Ronni, but it's the truth.

We walk together in silence to the elevator, watching for the doors to close before I said anything. She won't like what I have to tell her, but she needs to hear it.

"Sami, I'm worried about you."

"I know you are, but you have a lot to contend with already. Just," she sighs, "let me take this off your plate. It wasn't supposed to be there, anyway."

"Come on, don't be like that. I'm trying to help the only way I can without mom and dad around."

"El, you've always had my back, I know that, but you've always taken the brunt of everything at the detriment of yourself. I need you to be a little more of that selfish bachelor that you were before Gabby got sick, it will make me feel a lot better."

Before I can respond, the metal doors open and she shoots out into the atrium, making a sharp left toward the cafeteria. I follow at a leisurely pace until we get to the buffet line.

"Come on, Sam-squatch," I whisper in her ear, calling her my favorite nickname from our childhood. "I just want to make sure you aren't stressed out. I'll play better knowing that you and Gabby are okay."

"I'll be less stressed out if I'm not worried that you'll get traded somewhere between rounds of treatment," she shoots back at me.

"I'm not getting traded. Veronica is putting me on a huge list of events and interviews to improve my image. As long as nothing comes up between now and the end of the season, I'm good. There's still six months of the season ahead of me, and I'm watching my every move. We're fine."

She aims tired green eyes in my direction. I know better than to bullshit her, but I wasn't the one she needed to worry about. A nod of her head, looking an awful lot like our mother, and then she was turning away to gather more food on her plate. I hold my tongue, at least she was eating. Together, we wander through the lines as a team, as we always did; she went over to gather some fresh fruit, and I went to the drink cooler for the bottles of water and the iced coffee she likes. We meet back up at the register where we both stand with our phones at the ready to see who's tap to pay would register first. Call it sibling rivalry, or call it a tradition; no matter how mad we were about anything, we always set it aside for this. Together, we sit at a window booth and allow ourselves to relax for a moment.

"So, tell me more about this babysitter of yours." I should have known she would be the one to break the silence. She hated silence, she always said it gave too much space for thinking.

"I think you've run into her a few times before at events. Ronni—I mean Veronica—Snow."

Sami pauses, glancing at me. "You mean the intern that yelled at you last year when you showed up late to the benefit banquet? That one?" She laughs so hard tears pop up in her eyes. "Oh, El, you've got your hands full!"

"I know," I grumble, swiping a carrot stick from her tray.

"She still won't let me call her Ronni. She had to physically remove two models out of Wellsey's bed, and he can call her Ronni all day long. And I'm either Mr. Moxley or Elliot, but never Moxley or Mox. And I hate it when she calls me Mr. Moxley because it makes me sound like Dad."

"What have you done to prove that you can call her by her nickname, Elliot? Because I know you, and you probably have done nothing about it."

I pause on my way to swiping apple slices, staring hard at her. "Who says I did anything to her?" I reach forward for it, and she taps the back of my hand with her fingers.

"Come on, you act like I don't know you. You've probably done nothing outside of trying to charm your way out of trouble." Her head tilts in my direction, an eyebrow lifted. "I know I'm right."

"I don't think I like how certain you are." I swipe the apple slice I aimed for earlier, snagging it before she can get me. "I initiated a meeting with her this morning and I made it. So there!"

"Were you on time?"

"…No." I frowned. "I got waylaid by some young fans on my way there."

"Did you tell her you were going to be late?" I give her a look that confirms that I didn't call. "I see. And how did you apologize for being late?"

"Hold up, who's the responsible older sibling here? I missed the memo."

"See, this is what I'm talking about, bro. You need to do the responsible thing. Try making it up to her sometime, okay?"

"Yeah, yeah," I grumble, picking up my fork to eat real food.

We sit in silence for a bit, both of us focusing on eating before we could head upstairs. I stay with Sami and Gabby for another hour afterward, making sure that everything was situated with them before I headed back to my apartment alone. Maybe I needed to put some effort into this to get into Ronni's good graces, but I'd get there.

CHAPTER 6

VERONICA

THE BASS THUMPS in my skull and in counterpoint to my pulse, making me even more anxious. I lay my head against the wall, closing my eyes against the growing migraine that scratched just behind my eyeballs. Why in God's name Elliot thought that this was a great idea was truly beyond me. He'd been so good for the last two months, and now is when he lets loose? Like, seriously, there are only two games left before the All-Star break and instead of doing what every other meathead on the roster was doing—namely, resting, hydrating, and watching tapes of the upcoming teams–he was lounging in the VIP section of a club with God-knows-who and doing God-knows-what. A club that just opened, and had cameras everywhere, so it was a given that his face was plastered all over social media. Granted, it belonged to a former player, but it wasn't good, and it made me angry that of all the players to come in tonight, it was the one who doesn't need to be caught partying.

Forgive me, Father, I'm about to sin. I'm sorry for all the angry and obscene words I'm about to launch at this idiotic jock. In my defense, though, he had it coming.

I finish my water bottle, toss it in the nearby trash, and head to the velvet curtain. I'm certain he doesn't even know that I'm here right now. I only knew he was here because of social media tags blowing up my phone on the team socials. So much for my night in with a small tub of Ben and Jerry's and binging Lucifer reruns, I was stuck spending my night in the Sin Bin. As I approach the bouncer in front of Elliot, the big man steps in front of me.

"Sorry, sweetheart, he's off the clock and occupied," the giant rumbles over the music. I cross my arms over my chest and looked up at him, trying desperately to look intimidating. Or, as intimidating as 5-foot-6 can be next to someone a good foot taller than me. He looks down at me with a vaguely apologetic look while I glare up at him.

"Pity, because I'm about to have one hell of a workplace discussion with him about how this is screwing up my team algorithm. Now will you please get out of my way?" The stare-down continues, with him refusing to give me an inch, and I am in no mood to step back and play nice.

"Marco, let her in. That's my PR babysitter."

I see red. He's so going to hear about this. I'm over all of this. I'm over his playboy lifestyle, his immature antics, his irresponsibility. Over. It.

Marco the Mountain moves to his right, unlatching the velvet rope as he motions me forward. I stay still for a moment and just stare at Elliot. He sprawls across a couch, large arms stretched out across the back, swirling a rocks glass in one massive hand. The Ice Wolves hoodie he had on with his relaxed jeans should have looked out of place in a club like this, but somehow it didn't. That god-awful smirk of his is firmly in place, as always. He clearly didn't feel guilty about this at all. He broke our little stare-down and motions me forward with two fingers. On anyone other than him, that move would be the hottest thing known to humanity. On him, though, I…I can't deny it's still fetching. I just wished that the rest of him wasn't so abhorrent. I step just inside the rope so Marco can close off the VIP section again, but don't approach any farther.

There is no excuse, I know better, but I can't help it. His behavior trends, the way he looks at me right now, that I dropped everything that I needed to do for the last few months and he hadn't even bothered to help me fix his problems? I've had enough. I snap, seeing red.

"You know, for someone who is on the verge of getting traded, you sure aren't taking this seriously. I may have had plans other than dragging your ass out of a club for tonight."

"You had plans tonight, Snow Queen? With who?" He smiles wolfishly and winks at me, like he knows the truth. I bite my bottom lip just to keep the words inside. "Come on, come sit down for a few. I won't bite. Promise, I'll be on my best behavior."

"I highly doubt that 'best behavior' is something you're aware of." Despite that, I sit beside him, lean back against the couch and cross my arms across my chest. "This isn't helping your situation in the slightest, Moxley. Bottle service in a hot new club the night before a home game? The optics aren't great, my dude."

He looks over at me, opens his mouth to say something, and pauses. Eventually he restarts, "I'm aware, but I need a break. The stress is killing me. I can't do any better than what I have so far, but it doesn't seem to be enough. When is it ever going to be enough?"

In a way, he has been working hard for me recently. He attended back-to-back events without dropping his energy at all. I'm just frustrated because he's always underfoot.

"They want consistency and know this isn't just a one and done to check the boxes. We've got some, but not enough yet. We have to keep at it. Remember, you didn't get into this position by just one club event, and it's going to take more than one event to undo the damage." He leans forward, resting his elbows on his big knees and looking down at the half-full glass in front of him. A sigh escapes him as he bows his head. "I told you, this was going to be a long process, and we were stuck in this together. We're gonna have to keep this up through the post-season."

A growl rolls through him as he sits up. "Fine. Let me at least finish this like I promised Joey and then we can go. Here," he says, while pouring a fresh glass and handing it to me. "Let me guess, it would be 'bad optics' if I'm caught drinking alone, even if it is for branding, right?" His tone held some snark in it I don't appreciate, but I let that go.

Shaking my head, I take the proffered glass. I take a small sip, the chilled vodka going down smoothly with minimal burn. Whatever he's drinking, it isn't the cheap stuff. I watch him sip slowly as well. This will take forever, so I might as well settle in. I relax my posture a bit, sipping my drink again, and pull out my phone. I pop through the social media pages and look for problems, angry comments, and respond to some messages with one hand while sipping slowly from the other.

"Don't you ever get tired of being 'on' all the time? Like, what do you do for fun, Snow? This can't be everything you do."

My eyes dart to him, watching the way his eyes stay locked on me. Focused, driven. He wouldn't move on until he had the answer he was looking for. Breaking eye contact with him, I can't take how exposed I feel, like he can see my deepest secrets.

"I do more than babysit the social media! I also set up the locker room tours and the brew tastings on club level, and…"

His chuckle cut me off, and I glare at him. "I know you do that. But what do you do outside of work? What do you do for fun? All work and no play makes Snow a dull girl."

My head tilts in confusion. Is he trying to get to know me?

What is his deal? I poured some more into my glass. "I…I watch tv, or read. I spend time at the shelter outside the practice rink sometimes. There's not a lot of time left for me after I finish herding you boys around, though."

He frowns, his gaze turning dark at that. "You need to spend time for yourself, we're grown men that can take care of ourselves…"

I cut him off with a bark of laughter. "You can take care of yourselves? Mox, remember the incident with the rookie goalies? Or the time Jonesy had to send us out to get new street clothes because his luggage got lost and he didn't pack his backup set in his carryon? Or better yet, the time when I had to run interference so you could make it out of your hotel room and past the mob of girls who were stalking you in the lobby? No, there is no 'taking care of yourselves' at this point," I shake my head and chuckle, before sipping from my topped off glass. "The next time I get a call that one of you," I pause, waving a finger in his direction, "has done something stupid, I'll call you instead. You can do it for me. If I'm the Snow Queen," I wave my hand with a flourish, "then I decree it is so." A giggle escapes me at the idea.

His eyes widen a fraction, and his hand slowly covers his mouth. "Hey, Snow Queen…just how often do you go out for a drink?"

"I don't, I told you I barely have time for myself. Why are you asking such a stupid question….. oh," I sigh, slowly realizing that things are feeling fuzzy. "You got me drunk!" My anger from earlier tries to come back, but it wasn't the same. "Damnit, Mox, we have work tomorrow and I can't feel my face, and, and….." A giggle escapes me. "I think I'm drunk." I giggle again.

"Yeah, yeah, come on, let's get you home and in bed. Damned lightweight."

"I'm not, I'm…I'm…," I pause, sighing. "Yeah, maybe I am buzzy. It's all your fault, you know."

"My fault? I didn't go for the refill, that was all you, just saying."

He chuckles as he picks up my hand, helps me up to my feet, and then moves toward the velvet rope without letting go. I weave along behind him, trying to not acknowledge that he hasn't let go of my hand, or that the simple touch is making my belly flip. "It is most definitely your fault. If you wouldn't have gone out tonight, I wouldn't have had to follow you, then I wouldn't have been here, and I wouldn't be like this." I try to slip my hand from his, only for his large fingers to tighten down slightly.

"Hmm, fair point. How did you get down here? Uber?" He quickly pulls me against him and out of the path of a falling dancer beside us. My free hand smacks onto his chest and I have a split second to note the warmth I could feel through his team shirt and…did his heartbeat just speed up?

"Yeah, I live on the other side of town. Hey, slow down, not all of us are nine feet tall!" I'm nearly running to keep up with his long strides. We headed through a side door and emerge onto the dark sidewalk. I relaxed as the silence descended on us as the door clicked shut. I released a breath and looked toward his face. "Now what, big guy? We're outside in the cold."

He looks down, eyes widening in awareness that I stood in front of him without a coat. "Jesus, Ronni, I'm so sorry! Here, take this." He pulled his hoodie over his head, exposing a strip of toned abs as his t-shirt lifts as well. My mouth went dry as I took it in, while he finished pulling himself out of the material. I quickly darted my eyes away before he caught me gawking at him. "Come on, Snow, you're freezing. Here."

"Thanks," I murmur as I take the cloth from him and slip it over my head. It swallows me whole, which shouldn't be surprising with our size differences, but there is something comforting about it. And the smell, his woodsy cologne engulfing me as much as the hoodie did.

"Now, come on, let's get you home," he tells me while holding his phone to his head. "Hey, come around to the back entrance. I needed to make an escape." He pockets his phone before reaching out toward me, straightening the material of his shirt around me, and then grabbing a wrist. I gasp and pull away, but he just tightens his grip and grins. Winking at me, he rolls up the wrists, so they did not bury my hands. A black SUV stops beside us, and Elliot presses lightly on my back to guide me to the vehicle. He opens the door and ushers me in, before climbing in himself.

"Where to, sir?" Elliot studies me closely, silently telling me to give the driver my address.

"Oh, um….," I rattle off my address, confusion as to what we were doing. "Where are you going?" I whisper at Elliot, shooting him what I hope is an intimidating look.

"I'm taking you home. What does it look like?" He relaxes back onto the black leather seat, stretching his arms out along the back of the headrests and rolling his neck. "You didn't want to stay at the club, right? And I can't very well let you walk home like this. So I'm giving you a ride home."

What? The Actual. Hell?

My brain short-circuits as I replay what he just said. He's taking me home. I mean, it isn't a huge secret really where anyone lived as far as the players went; we coordinated the ride service for them prior to events regularly. But my house? No one came there. Hell, I hardly stuck around long, and it was my place.

I blink my eyes slowly, as my alcohol soaked brain tried to figure out what the hell he just said. "I'm a big girl, I can get there myself."

"I'm sure you are, but just humor me. I want to make sure you get there."

"Whatever," I grumble as I crossed my arms. I struggle to not close my eyes as his cologne envelopes me and I feel my eyelids droop. I lean back against the seat, trying desperately to ignore just how close his hand was to me. The surrounding silence is surprisingly comfortable, and without thinking about it, my eyes closed against the lights of the city.

43

CHAPTER 7

VERONICA

"COME ON, Snow Queen, we gotta go inside."

His voice is muffled, and feels like I'm hearing it coming from inside my head. Wait...am I? I sit up, and realize with some mortification that I am hearing it inside my head because my ear is pressed against Elliot Moxley's very large, very warm chest. Setting my hand down on the seat to lift myself, I find myself not with a handful of cushion, but a jean-clad thigh that is clenching under my touch.

Jesus. Get a grip, girl! I think, immediately followed by, *don't mind if I do!* Clearly, the angel and devil on my shoulders are busy at work tonight. *It's just the alcohol talking, just be cool.*

His large hand wraps around mine gently, lifting it off of his leg and slowly pulling me toward the door. I follow him, still fuzzy from the drinks and the momentary lapse in consciousness in the vehicle. I trudge along, weaving slightly. *Why is he so completely sober? It's not fair.*

We get to my door, my hand never leaving his. I reach into my pocket for my key with my free hand, only for him to slip it from my numb fingers. He smoothly opens the door and walks in, pulling me inside behind him.

"Mox, what..." I shake my head in confusion as he makes

himself at home, going into my kitchen and coming back with a bottle of water.

"Drink this. You have the smallest couch known to humanity, you know that?"

"Well, yeah, no one comes here. I barely come here." I glance sullenly at the lone loveseat in my living room. "Thank you for getting me inside, but we have a long day tomorrow…"

"Not so fast, Snow Queen. My mother would skin me if she knew I left a friend in an unsafe position. I got you sloshed, now I'm going to fix it. So, where's your pain meds? And goodness, do you have crackers? Bread? Anything to eat in this place?"

That confirms it. I am having a lucid dream and Moxley is a pod person. "I always grab from the deli outside the arena. Again, not home long enough. Remember that whole conversation about babysitting the team?"

His green eyes on me that are way sharper than they should have been for this time of night after bottle service in a bar. "Fine. I'm getting you food in the morning. Can you make it to bed okay?" He slowly ushered me down the hall, following behind me as I walked into my bedroom and face planted on my bed, bouncing gracelessly off the blankets. "Come on, Cinderella, let's take the shoes off first at least. Need a hand?"

All I can do is grunt out a muffled sound, his large hands on my ankle, working to untie my shoes. It's the last thing I recall before sleep pulled me down into unconsciousness.

***

Morning came far too early for my liking and brought all the regrets from the previous night with it. My head was pounding, my tongue felt like sandpaper, and there was something large against my back…that wasn't my pillow.

"Oh, God…" I moan, trying to sit up. I freeze as realization hit me that there was what felt suspiciously large arm wrapped around my waist.

"Not yet, Ma, five more minutes," a deep, gravelly voice huffs behind me, warm air tickling my ear.

"Um…Mox?" He grunts into my hair, before sighing, his warm breath making me shiver. Jesus, the man sleeps like the dead! "Mox, why are you in my bed, and why are you spooning me?"

"Couch was too small, and you started it. You big-spooned me first. I was just going to stay on this side of the bed before you went full starfish and took up the whole thing. It was a case of 'spoon or be spooned,' or worse, catch these hands." Looking down, I could see my wrists held loosely in one large hand.

"Okay," I say slowly, while trying to shift from under his arm. "So, do you think you can un-spoon me so we can go to work? We have places to get to and," I check my phone on the nightstand, "roughly an hour to make it happen." His groan vibrates through my back, and I feel him shift before stretching out. I shiver at the loss of his body heat and attempt to roll off my side of the bed without hurling, the pounding and swirling in my head growing stronger as I got more vertical. "Oh, God, I swear I'm never doing this again," I moan as I dropped my head between my knees.

"Here, take this." I slowly lift my head and look into the face of Elliot, kneeling before me, holding out a bottle of water and ibuprofen for me. "Get some of this in you, and we'll snag breakfast on the way inside the arena if you can handle it. Okay?" My stomach flipped at the idea of consuming anything, but I do as I was told. I quickly toss back the pills and sip the water. "Good girl."

My eyes shoot back open, wondering if he even realized what he had said. It hurt too much to think about, so I get up slowly. I have to get myself put together before I show up at work, and I just wanted to go back to bed.

"Um, the bathroom is over there if you want to clean up. Oh God, what are you wearing to work? You can't go to work in what you slept in!"

He chuckles at me, plucking at the rumpled t-shirt. "Snow, I change when I get to the arena, anyway. No one is going to see this, really. But yeah, I'm going to go that direction. Our ride will be here in 30, okay?" I groan and close my eyes, and he laughs as he walks out the door.

I look down, and note that I still had his hoodie on over my jeans and shirt from last night. He only took off my shoes the night before, I note with amazement. It was considerate. I slowly pull the large shirt over my head and set it aside, before escaping into my closet for a change of clothes, finding a pair of jeans and one of my own Ice Wolves hoodies to wear. I can hear him in the living room on his phone as I stepped into the hallway, making a run for the bathroom.

The mirror told me what I already knew; I look rough, but I had to get somewhat presentable. Getting dressed, I attempt to put myself together, and head out to join him in the living room.

"I know it hurts, but you need to do it. You'll feel better afterward, I promise. I know, Princess. I know. Just," he sighs, listening, "please, just do it for me? Okay? Atta girl. Okay, I gotta jet. Yeah, I'll see you after practice. Send me what to bring over for lunch. Yeah, it's a date. Love you too, Princess. Bye."

I freeze. He spent the night at my house, laying on the other side of my bed, spooning against me, and he was calling some other girl Princess? Did she know what he was up to last night? I had no right to be jealous, but how could he do that to someone else? I should have known that his "trying to clean up the bad boy image" was just an act, really.

I grit my teeth and entered the living room watching him slide his phone into his pocket as he looks out my window. I cough lightly, watching as he jumps and turns to face me.

"Hey, our ride's here. Are you ready to go?" He seems so cool and calm, like he wasn't just standing in my living room and talking to his…girlfriend? Not a wife, he just had a super public breakup last season.

"Yeah, let's go."

Our ride to the arena is quiet, with both of us engrossed in our phones. As we pull up to the arena, Elliot opens the door and holds his hand out for me. I shakily climb out of the car and walk away toward the press entrance, slightly aware of the handful of kids outside the entrance that scream his name as he heads to the opposite door.

I leave him behind, listening to him chat with the kids, being charming as ever. The questions they asked about what he was doing, how does practice work, came at him from all sides, but he answered them all patiently.

Glancing at my watch as I approached the doors, I notice he's going to be late to his own warmups, but I don't feel like saving him. I can't help but feel that whatever lukewarm feelings he gave me when he took care of me last night, had been killed this morning by being a sneaky bastard.

CHAPTER 8

ELLIOT

MY HEAD still feels a little fuzzy from the last night; I knew I shouldn't have been at the club on the night before a game — especially knowing that the only difference between a game night and a school night is the volume of work and yelling that ensues when you don't get enough sleep. I didn't sleep that great, but I couldn't just leave Ronni alone in that state. I should've stopped her before her last glass, but to be honest, I was glad I wasn't alone anymore.

Certainly, I could have called a couple of the boys in to hang with me. It would have been great for Joe's club, but it wasn't an official event, this was just doing a favor for a good friend, no appearance fees or anything. Joe was the one who helped me get situated as a rookie before he retired the following season. It was the least I could do, sitting on a couch and being a low-key draw for his publicity. If I called anyone else, they would end up needing contracts and appearance fees, and that just wasn't necessary for me.

Staying over at her house really wasn't part of the plan either, but I felt bad for getting her to that point and then leaving her stranded. Waking up against her, with my nose buried in her hair and my arm around her frame, that was also not at all in the plan. Quite the opposite, really, but I can't say I was upset by it. It was surprisingly…nice. Comfortable, relaxing, even. There were no preconceived plans, it just was. It was refreshing compared to the Instagram-ready poses from my past relationships. And if I'm totally honest with myself, having Ronni drop her Snow Queen façade for a moment gave me a whole new insight into what she was truly like.

She isn't a horrible person, she just doesn't pull any punches with me. It's never been a secret how she felt about me. She thinks I'm a man-whore party boy who exists to cause one publicized nightmare after another. Last year definitely looked like it, but that was then. I've bent over backwards for her so far this season to do everything she asked, and at most I get a cool acknowledgment that I did something average. Perhaps it's that reason that I keep wanting to do better, try harder for her. She is the one that can help me save my career here, and it's her word at the end that may save me.

Speaking of Ronni…I curse as I cringed. I forgot I promised her breakfast and coffee. I saw one of the equipment assistant interns in the hall and flag him down. With specific instructions jotted in his phone and a fifty for the food and delivery, he raced toward the exit and I headed back toward the locker room. Leaning against my locker for a second my eyes drifted close, and I tried to slow down my brain. I needed to focus on practice, and I couldn't waste time today.

It was appointment day for Gabby. I have never missed one, I've been her constant since her diagnosis last year. No one knew, but that was where I spent a lot of my free time, and also why my schedule looked the way it did. My sister does what she can for her, but as a single mom, it was rough. That was why I stepped in early in her illness, so Sami could focus on Gabby's care and not worry about the bills. My schedule is lighter in the summer, and when I'm not on the road during the season, so I help where I can. I had finally convinced her to quit her job when I started getting my bigger checks, but I'm still Gabby's go to when things are scary.

"How did Joe's event go last night, Mox?" I looked over at our veteran goalie, Val. He played with Joe as well in his early days. It was nice to know that friendships extended past the limits of the contracts and the game.

"It was good, I hope it helped. How's that shoulder feeling?"

I should've known better than to change the subject. He grinned at me, and I knew by looking at him he just scented blood.

"The shoulder is fine. But not as fine as you were apparently feeling last night with Ronni."

"Say again?" He said nothing, just whipped his phone out with a picture of Ronni and I, with my hand low on her back as I ushered her through the crowd. I didn't actually touch her that low...or did I? The angle of the shot clearly made it look like I had crossed the line from socially acceptable to exceedingly intimate.

Fuck. She's going to lose it when she sees this.

"Damnit, it's not what it looks like." I shake my head and hand the phone back to him. She's going to have my hide for this, I just knew it.

"Really? Because it kind of looks like you weren't just drumming up business for a good friend, El."

"I know, I know," I grumble. "But everything was legitimate. I promise. Nothing happened."

"You're still in photos in questionable positions with a woman," he warns, while adjusting his skates. "Again."

"This is different, she isn't Lacey. She did nothing on purpose. If anything, I should've paid more attention to our surroundings, I had a clearer head than she did."

"You got her drunk?" The words hiss between his

clenched teeth as he grabs a handful of my jersey. "What the fuck, dude?"

"No," I counter. "She shared the bottle service with me. When I noticed it was hitting her harder, I got her out of there and took her back to her place since I had car service. She wasn't in good shape by the time we got there, so I," I pause. "I spent the night at her place," I add quietly.

Bishop stares, looking at me like I grew three heads. Cursing under his breath, dragging me by my jersey to the attached trainer room. "You didn't." He groans, dropping his head into his hands. "Jesus, Mox, did you even ask her for permission first?"

"She really wasn't in any shape to take care of herself last night. She passed out in the car on the way there. I couldn't just leave her there like that. What if she got sick? What if she hurt herself trying to walk around? I told her when we got there, and she walked in on her own two feet. I made sure she had water and made it to bed. I didn't touch her, I didn't even touch her clothes. And this morning we talked about it on the way to the arena."

"Mox, man, you do the dumbest things being a good guy, you know that?"

I nodded. "Yeah, I know."

CHAPTER 9

TODAY WAS GOING to be the worst day ever. My head was pounding, I was late; I feel dehydrated, and I kind of need food. At that thought, my stomach flips, and I shudder. Okay, maybe not food.

Bolting from the SUV, I nearly run to the PR offices just to clock in on time. I had made it to my desk with minimal distractions, thankfully. I sigh in relief and relax for a moment, but then curse as I realize that not only did I show up to work with mismatched socks, but I also did not get to stop at the deli and get my coffee and muffin. It's all his fault, if it wasn't for him I wouldn't have forgotten, or ran late.

With a groan, I set my head on my desk, pillowing my head on my forearms. I don't want to leave to go back out and get anything, but ordering from an app is barely dependable with as large as the building is. I could always make do with a K-Cup and pray that there's enough creamer left in the press fridge for me.

My stomach lurches at the thought, or maybe it was just hunger. I'll have to deal with this somehow. I've almost convinced myself to get up and make the trek outside in the cold when…

"Ms. Snow?" I turn toward the doorway to see a young man, clearly uncomfortable in new surroundings, standing just inside our office. He was wearing the Ice Wolves polo shirt that most of the physical therapy and equipment teams preferred, but he appears to be far younger than the specialists I'm accustomed to seeing around the arena. He must be an intern. There is a bag and a coffee carrier in his hand, but it looks like he doesn't know what to do with it.

"That's me. What's up?" I stand slowly, smoothing my hands down my wrinkled jeans, and make my way towards him.

"I'm supposed to give you these with a message," he replies, handing me the treats and then pulling a phone out of his back pocket. "Um…this is a direct quote. 'I'm sorry I was a complete asshole this morning and forgot to feed you. I'll make sure that I never ever do that again. Promise! Thanks for last night. Mox,'" he recites from the screen before looking over at me. "Should I say anything back to him if he asks?"

I peer inside the bag to find the same muffin I had during our last coffee meeting, and looking at the scribbles on the coffee cup confirms that they are also my usual order. How did he know? Did he actually pay attention?

Looking back up at the intern, I smiled. "Tell Mr. Moxley thanks, but the next time he needs to apologize it should be in person. Thank you for bringing this, you really saved my morning!"

He nods and runs back out the door, leaving me to bask in the scent of fresh roasted coffee and warm baked goods. Why is it that every time I'm determined to keep him in his bad boy box, he redeems himself? It doesn't make up for the potential girlfriend on the phone issue, nor the fact he stayed over in my apartment without permission, but perhaps he's a decent guy, anyway.

"What's that?" Jessica's head pops over the cubicle wall,

and her eyes go wide as she sees the bag in front of me. "Hey, how did you get a coffee fairy? That's not fair!"

"The traumatized intern that just left ran it in for me," I say as I put a straw into my coffee. "Mox forgot to stop for breakfast before we ran into the arena this morning..." I freeze as I realize what I said and how it sounded.

"Mox? You're on a shortened name basis with him now?" Her chuckle makes me close my eyes and groan. "Oh, come on, Ronni, it's cute how you still try to act mad about this whole setup, you know."

"Yeah yeah, I know, but can we attempt to be professional about it? He used a poor underpaid intern to do his bidding, and then delivers an apology where he refers to himself as an asshole. That's hardly appropriate and you know it."

"Whatever. The real question is, why did he owe you breakfast this morning?" her voice going higher as her eyebrows waggle at me. "Wait. Was it bad? Is this forgiveness breakfast? Oh, Ronni, that's horrible!"

"We are not discussing this, Jess," I laugh. "At least, we are not discussing this in the middle of the office. And on that note, I need to teach a jock how to apologize."

I walk off, my fresh coffee in hand, and try to make sense of these conflicting ideas in my head.

CHAPTER 10

ELLIOT

I MAKE it out to the ice for practice, dodging questions and stares from my teammates along the way. This was where I felt at home. With the whisper of blades on the ice, the crack of sticks and pucks, I could regain my center. I don't need yoga for that. After a few warm up laps and practice shots on goal, I drop to my knees and start stretching.

"Hey, Moxley." Her voice isn't loud, but I could hear it over the din of practice. I spun on the ice to face where she's standing along the bench, before settling deeper into the stretch. I shoot a cocky grin at her that hopefully doesn't give away the fact that my thighs are tight as hell after sleeping on her bed.

"Hey yourself, Snow Queen. How was breakfast?" Her blush and ducking her head tells me everything I need to know, but I'm dying to hear her say it.

"That's why I'm here. Thank you, you didn't have to, and I imagine you have a traumatized intern running around here somewhere. I appreciate it. You even got my order right!"

I grin at her. *Nailed it!* "Anytime, Snow Queen, but I promise next time I won't forget your coffee."

Her face tightens a bit, and the smile doesn't totally get to her eyes. Okay, maybe she's sensitive about that part. She bites her bottom lip and looks down at the ice for a moment before making eye contact again.

"Well, I don't plan on drinking with you, like, ever again, so you don't have to worry about it. I actually came down here to ask you something. A team favor, actually."

"Go for it," I say as I drop my knees a little wider and grimace as my muscles complain. *This sucks*, I think as I contemplate how much time with the team's physical therapist I might need later.

"So, there's a surprise visit coming up for the children's hospital tomorrow and they'd like to coordinate a few sports celebrity visitors. There are representatives coming from every other organization, and we were going to send Barker, except he's now on concussion protocol and unavailable. Can you swing an impromptu visit? It would look great for you, and may help upstairs as well."

Tomorrow. There's a chance Gabby might still be there, but there's no saying I'll be on oncology's floor if I did. It's a gamble, sure, but worth it either way. "Sounds great. So show up and hand out some toys then? Do I need to bring anything?"

She clears her throat like she's uncomfortable. "Well, if you want to bring your favorite Sharpie along for autographs, go for it. Um, I could always get a pass for your girlfriend-"

"My who?" I haven't had a girlfriend all season, why does she think I have one now?

"Your girlfriend. Princess Buttercup, you just talked to her this morning, and at the coffee shop the other day."

I full-on belly laugh at her. "You thought that she," he gasps, "my girlfriend? Oh, Snow Queen…no. No girlfriends. I've been a good boy so far this season."

"I don't care who you date, or even if you date, as long as

you keep your nose clean this time. Remember, that's our goal here. Clean up your reputation."

"So, does that mean you don't want to know that you're the only one I've shared a bed with since May?" Her cheeks burned red and even though I knew I was being antagonistic with her, I can't quite stop myself. "I can be a good boy when I want to be." I grin and wink. "I could be a very good boy, if you want me to be." Her mouth drops open and her eyes go wide.

"Mr. Moxley, that's—"

"What, Snow Queen, that's unprofessional? That's not appropriate? That doesn't apply here?" I drop my hips back and rock. I know what this looks like to outsiders, but between my knotted muscles and her feelings broadcasting across her face, I can't stop this train now. I can't help poking the bear just a little more.

"You are impossible, you know that, right?" She shakes her head with her eyes closed, as though that will shake the image out of her head. "So meet me here tomorrow at one, get there at 1:30. There will be a small luncheon with some patients, and then we'll make the rounds at 3 sharp to the patients who couldn't make it. Some pictures, some video clips, and then you're done. Sounds good?"

I nod, and mentally make a note to check in on Gabby if she's still up there. Surely I can sneak away or convince her to play that she doesn't know me. Easier said than done, I'm sure, she thinks I walk on water; she says technically I do, it's just frozen first.

"Sounds great. I'll see you then, Ms. Snow," I call out, winking at her before grinning. She turns away, but not before I catch her lips lifting into a smile. Busted.

I chuckle as I continue to loosen up, and turn back towards the rest of my teammates on the ice. I make eye contact with Bishop, who raises his eyebrow at me in question. *What was that about?* I can tell he's saying. I shake my head, the universal sign for nothing. He smirks back at me, clearly not believing me. The disadvantage of knowing your teammate so well that you can have a conversation wordlessly on the ice? They know what you're saying without actually saying anything.

"Don't look at me like that," I grovel, giving him a side eye. "She's fixing my screwups. Least I can do is get her coffee occasionally."

He snorts at me, and grins. "Sure, Mox, that really sounded like just getting her coffee for fixing your screw ups," he chuckles. "She's a good person, don't screw this up, okay? It took forever to get her comfortable around the locker room. It would be nice to not start from scratch."

"There's nothing to screw up, man. I'm being a good boy. I'm not going to shit where I eat, I need this team too much." I was a really good boy this morning when I woke up pressed against her…yeah, not thinking about that part.

I can tell he doesn't really believe me, but he lets it go, shifting on his skates to go toward the goal. I move through the rest of my warm up, and take some practice shots at the net. The whole time, I mull over what he's said. What does he think I'm doing with her outside of work?

I go through the motions of practice and mull over what Bishop insinuated. The last thing I need is for the head office or HR to think we were inappropriate. The scariest part, if anyone knew I spent the night at her house last night—and that was definitely all that happened between us—it would most likely destroy my redemption and her career. I have to talk to her, hopefully before anything gets said anywhere that goes upstairs.

After practice, I skip the shower, throw my team shirt and joggers on, and slip on my sneakers. I don't even take the time to lace them before I'm barreling out the door and heading toward her office.

She's sitting at her desk, focused on the screen and fingers tapping out a rapid fire message on her keyboard, earbuds in, and I can tell she isn't aware of me or anything else around her. Still, I had to try getting her attention. I called her name and get zero response. I sigh, I don't want to do this, but…

I set my hand lightly on her shoulder, and cringe as she screeches, startled, and misses the edge of the chair. Before she could fall, I shoot forward and hold her upright, saving her from a bruised tailbone I'm sure. However, what I can't help but notice is how well my hands fit along her sides.

Fuck, I'm in big trouble.

"You good, Snow?" I say as she rips a headphone out of her ear.

"Jesus, Moxley, what were you thinking?" She hisses the words between gritted teeth, her eyes still wide. I try desperately to not notice how her hands are fisting in my shirt, her nails digging through the material into my shoulders — and, why have I never noticed how much I liked that?

"I tried to get your attention. We need to talk." I hold on to her until she gets her feet under her and then smoothes out her top with shaky hands. She shoots a look in my direction that I couldn't totally read, but I had a feeling it meant she didn't really want to discuss anything with me at the moment.

"What is there to talk about? Thanks for breakfast, and making sure I made it home okay last night. We're good," she says, her forehead creased in confusion.

I scrub a hand along my jaw, thinking before I answer. "So, Bishop pointed out that maybe it wasn't the most appropriate course of action for me. For anything yesterday, especially since the club pics are up with us in them. If I overstepped, I'm sorry."

"So because someone else, who wasn't there last night, has opinions on how we handled last night as adults, you're now apologizing?"

"It wasn't appropriate for me to spend the night, or—"

She slapped a hand across my mouth mid-word, causing my next inhale to be her citrusy lotion. I could feel my eyes drift close as I took in that scent that drove me crazy all night.

"Come with me." Her words were cold, but the hand that grabs mine is scorching. Without another word, she pulls me down the hall into the press room, shoving me through the door before quietly shutting the door behind us. "Do you want everyone to find out? Saying it out there will guarantee they'll all know what happened last night."

"But nothing happened last night."

"You know that. I know that. No one else does. But if the PR staff catch wind? Everyone will think they know or assume something. And do we really want to know what the head office will say after that?"

That made sense, and it sucked that I didn't think about it. I ran a hand through my hair and released a frustrated breath. Focus, Mox, focus.

"Okay, sorry. I didn't think that one through. Um…Let me make it up to you? Dinner after Saturday's game?"

"We can't go anywhere that late. Not without questionable visuals."

"Come by my place after the press conference. I make a mean burger." I hold a breath and pray that her answer would be yes.

She looks up into my face, and I feel like she's sizing me up for how serious I'm taking this. "Fine. I'll come by after the game. For dinner. That's it."

"Perfect. I'll see you then."

With a quick glance back to her, I step out the door and close it softly behind me, then break into a jog to put some distance between us.

CHAPTER 11

VERONICA

I SHOULDN'T BE HERE. I really shouldn't. I look down at the bag in my hand, with the two bottles of red wine and cheesecake, the bottles clinking cheerily against each other as the elevator continued its upward trajectory. It's too late to back out now. In roughly 10 seconds the doors are going to open onto Elliot's floor, and then maybe 15 seconds after that I'll be at his door.

It's fine. Everything will be fine, I tell myself again as I knock on the door. Elliot opens the door, looking relaxed in bare feet, relaxed jeans and a black t-shirt. He grins widely and holds the door open.

"I brought desert and wine, I didn't know if you had anything," I said as I handed over the bag to him.

"Thanks, I'll put the wine in the fridge for a bit. Make yourself comfortable, dinner is almost done."

I drop my purse on the entryway table before following him into his spacious kitchen, taking in his surroundings. The brushed steel island countertop has two place settings prepared already. I take in the clean lines of the appliances before seeing him bend over to put the bottle in the fridge's bottom.

Dear Lord, thank you for that ass! Stop that, Ronni!

I quickly glance away before he can notice and sit down on the stool by one plate.

"Can I get you a drink? I have water, beer, and a bottle of white already chilled, I think."

"White's fine," I reply with a smile, and watch as he brings over a bottle and two glasses, sitting down beside me and pouring carefully. We eat, sharing some small talk between bites. Surprisingly, it's enjoyable, and the silence isn't uncomfortable.

"So, if you weren't babysitting a bunch of grown men-children, what would you do with your life?" The question seems to come out of left field and surprises me.

"Media marketing is what I went to school for, so I guess I technically went to school to learn how to babysit the social media of a man-child like you," I chuckle, before taking a sip of wine. "I guess this is what I always wanted to do, I just didn't realize it was going to be as much…handling."

I groan internally because "handling" and other double-entendres and that is totally not what we need right now. We can have a full conversation without that, I know we can. We're grownups.

He stares into his wineglass, that dimple on full display as he tries not to laugh. "Yeah, I suppose a few of us do require extra…handling. I should apologize for that, but it's really fun to watch you squirm sometimes."

I rolled my eyes and took another sip of wine. "Of course you'd think it was funny to get me worked up, you've made a sport of it the last couple seasons."

"No, it wasn't quite like that. It's just…you can't see your face when I call you Snow Queen, you know? It's just fun. And when you give as good as you get, it's hard not to pass up the chance."

"I'm not your personal plaything, Elliot, I don't exist solely for your entertainment."

"I'm aware, but can you say you don't kind of like it a little." And there's that dimpled grin again. "It makes work fun, right?"

"Fine, you're right, it's kind of fun to egg you on." I smile back. "Have you ever contemplated the strangeness of our, I don't know, friendship? Like, we get along now."

He tops off our glasses while I think about it. He isn't wrong; we have built a comfortable friendship of sorts out of this forced proximity. While we may not be greatest friends, we're at least amicable.

"We do," he agrees. "I have to admit, when Coach first put us together I thought this was the worst idea ever, because of how we interacted last season. I prepared myself for a season of torture and torment, and that I would be damn lucky to finish with my contract still in one piece. Instead, I feel like it's breathing new life into my career. I always enjoy going for ice time, but now I actually like the off-ice time, too."

My heart jumps at that, and I just stare at him in awe. There was so much more to him than everyone gave him credit for. Hell, there was more to him than even I did, and I could feel my chest tighten as I feel the guilt wash over me. Have I been shortchanging him this entire time? I look him in the eye and sensed that I'm truly seeing him clearly for the first time. He's not as "bad boy" as he's been portrayed.

CHAPTER 12

ELLIOT

"STAND RIGHT HERE, MR. MOXLEY." The photographer, some hipster dude, has been repeating the same line of directives for the last hour. Stand here, move here, move like this, and so on. I stand against a glaring white backdrop, one of the latest team shirts stretched across my chest, leaning against my stick, my hand wrapped around the tape on my blade. It's supposed to be a relaxed pose, but I'm anything but. I felt like a spring that has been compressed too far, and I'm about to explode. I had to focus and unclench my jaw, put my practiced "boy next door" smile in place, and moved as I was told.

Off to the side I saw Ronni, phone in her hand, taking photos and videos of the shoot for team social media posts. She had told me she would be here to do this, and to put the good boy optics on the team sites, as well as for my own. I owe her big time, because she's always there for me and getting the content that is improving the head office's opinion of me.

After a few more clicks of the camera, swapping props, and throwing an assortment of hoodies and team wear on,

Hipster Guy says I needed to go change into the suit in the next room for the higher end photos.

Whatever, I just wanted this done already.

I stalk towards the door, hoping to get this over with sooner as opposed to later. Closing the door behind me, I let loose the breath that I didn't realize I had been holding. I drop bonelessly onto the bench near the vanity, close my eyes, and just breathe. I hear the door click open behind me quietly and brace myself for more demands from the styling team.

"Mox? Are you okay?"

Hearing Ronni's voice was the last thing that I actually expected. Startled, I turned toward her and then cringed as she shrunk back toward the door.

"Hey. Sorry, I wasn't expecting you. Come on in."

"You looked a little upset out there, and not quite your-self." She shuts the door behind her and leans against it. "I can reschedule this if you need. There's no reason to push the issue if you aren't okay, we might even get a different photog-rapher. I mean, it'll be hard this short of notice but if you aren't feeling it-"

"No, no it's fine. I'm just," I pause with a sigh, "Yeah, I guess I'm not feeling this today. I just want to get this over with so I can escape, you know what I mean?" I grimace. "It's not that I'm not appreciative of the team picking me as the face of the organization, it's an honor. Really. But I've never really been 100% comfortable being on display like this and for this long at a time."

She cringes and then nibbles on her bottom lip. I grit my teeth against a groan, so she won't find out that it drives me batshit crazy when she does that.

"I can see how to speed this up. The schedule only shows this portion of the shoot left, so maybe if this goes fast you can get out before dinner?"

I grab her hand and place a soft kiss on her palm. "Thanks, Snow Queen. Where would I be without you?"

Her breath stutters as she looks up at me. "You would probably be in a lot more trouble than you are now, Mox."

"Who's saying I'm not already," I murmur, pulling her close. My heart races. This could go oh so right, or oh so wrong.

She catches herself against my chest with her hand splayed across the lapel over my heart. Her eyes shoot up to mine, wide and slightly unfocused. The tip of her tongue slipped out to wet her lips, and that's it.

Game over. I am hopelessly lost.

I don't even recall dropping my head down toward hers, or wrapping my hand around the back of her head, but there we are. Our breaths mingle together and I take in the way her eyelashes flutter against her cheeks, before closing the last of the distance between us.

Fireworks. I could feel them, I heard them; I wanted more. My hand that still had a hold of her wrist let go to wrap around her waist, pulling her taught against me. A whimper escapes her lips, and I just needed to have more. Just more. Sliding the tip of my tongue lightly along the seam of her lips, I coax them open lightly. Her lips quirk up at my press, but then I feel her tongue slip out to touch mine.

I'm drowning in her. Jesus, if this is heaven, I never want to come back to earth. This is better than winning the Stanley Cup, MVP, and my first-round draft pick. Nothing can top this, ever. Or, at least that's the last thought I have before I feel her nails at the back of my skull and I lose track of all coherent thought. My brain goes fuzzy and I swear I can feel all the blood in my body drop south.

"Fuck, Ronni, baby," I whisper against her lips before diving back in again for another taste. Her fingernails are magic, her lips are nirvana, and I couldn't suck in a full breath if I tried. Slowly, I pull back, resting my forehead against hers, panting like I've skated stingers for an hour. "I want...I can't...here..." My brain is racing and I can't string a sentence together no matter how hard I try.

"Yeah, I know," she whisper back, her breath teasing across my lips. "We'll talk about this after, okay?" She shifts her feet to step away from me. "But first you have to let go."

Reluctantly, I loosen my fingers from where it had somehow clenched onto the back of her shirt, and step back. I will myself to control my breathing and slide my damp palms shakily down my thighs. When did I start shaking? The air in my lungs burns as I try to breathe my way back to normal.

"Okay, so, how much longer am I their trained monkey, Snow?" I need to know. Now. I need to know how much longer I have to keep my hands to myself.

"You've got about another hour, maybe. It shouldn't take too long."

I nod, and start to walk out the door and pause. "Um, can you stall them for a couple minutes? I need a few," I chuckle and glance down, then stifle a harder laugh when I see her eyes go wide.

"Um, yeah, no problem." She slips out the door first, but not before I see her take a subtle second glance back at me. "See you in a few, Mox."

I don't know what I've gotten myself into but I'm not mad about it.

CHAPTER 13

VERONICA

OH. My. God.

Elliot "Who Taught Him To Kiss Like That" Moxley just kissed me. No, not kissed. I was pretty sure he just swallowed my soul, and the only skin-to-skin contact he had was his mouth on mine and a hand in my hair.

There is a buzzing in my head and I don't know what to think. I can still feel him against my lips, and the light burn of his stubble. I lift a shaky hand to my lips and trace a finger over my bottom lip, as I consider saving this as a core memory.

As I make my way from the dressing room back to the set, panic bubbles up in my chest. This is a HR nightmare. This wasn't supposed to happen, and this had serious repercussions on both of us. His reputation couldn't take another hit like having a relationship with a coworker, and how can I expect to keep moving up the Ice Wolves's organizational ladder with "made out with the team captain" hanging over my head?

But...it wasn't bad. If I'm totally honest with myself, I actually kind of liked it. A lot. I'd love to experience more of that if it won't kill me. But I can't jeopardize our careers or the plans for this season! I slump down in the director's chair that was set up in the corner for me, and watch for Elliot to come back out. I hope no one noticed anything between us and reported back. My gut clenches as I considered that. It wouldn't be the first time that idle gossip ruined something because of the shadow of doubt about a couple of co-workers.

The door banged open, and Elliot came out of the room, striding across the set like a predator. The long, lean lines of his legs stretching the pants arrest my attention. Good Lord, it's not fair that he looks that freaking good in a suit!

"Let's get this show on the road, okay? I'm sure you all have better places to be than hanging out with me." From anyone else, that statement would label someone hard to work with. From him, it just gave off this self-deprecating charm like he's not worth the effort. It was equal parts sweet and sad that he felt like that.

A flurry of activity erupted around him, as makeup and hair assistants swarmed, but the entire time, despite the conversations happening around him, his eyes never left me. I widened my eyes at him in the universal sign of "knock it off," only for him to smirk at me and wink. Withholding the urge to roll my eyes back at him, I groan; I swear, if I keep rolling my eyes I'll get a cramp or they'll freeze like that.

My phone began buzzing in my hand, and I squeak as I watch it tumble from my slack fingers to the floor. Please don't break, I pray as I bend down to pick it up, releasing a tight breath as I see my screen is still intact. Of course I can't totally relax as I saw Jessica's name on the screen.

"Hi," I wheeze, coughing slightly before trying again, "hi, Jess. What's up?"

"Just touching base. You're at the photo shoot with Moxley, right?" Panic. Sheer panic. I stop breathing, my head feeling fuzzy. "Ronni, are you still there?"

"Um, yeah," I mutter. "Where are you right now? Do you have a second?"

"Absolutely! What's up?" Her chipper voice did nothing to soothe my rattled nerves.

"Work wife privileges. I have to tell you something, and you absolutely cannot tell another soul. I don't know what to do!"

"You've got it, chica, but you're kind of scaring me, are you okay?"

"Yes, no, I don't know." I laughed. "Mox kissed me."

Silence. "What?"

I sighed, then repeated, "Mox kissed me. One second we were talking and the next he had his lips on mine and his hands in my hair, and I didn't stop him and honestly...," I trail off. "I don't think I wanted to stop him either."

"Oh my God, Ronni. He's the talent! We're supposed to handle their social media, we're not supposed to handle them like that!"

"I know! What do I do now?" I twist a loose curl around my fingers and look over at Elliot again. "HR will have a heyday if they find out this happened."

"So don't tell anyone? Seriously, as much of a rule follower as we both are, I think you've earned a 'get out of jail free' card. You could do so much worse for yourself, really."

I pull my phone away from my head to look at the screen again, because did she really say what I think she said? She's cool with this? "Really?"

"Yes, really! I mean, in the last couple months, how has he treated you? He's been a perfect gentleman toward you, even if he's up to no good with everyone else." I gnaw nervously on my bottom lip as I glanced back at the shoot. "Honestly, what is the worst that can happen? You hate it and he ends up traded, eventually. Or, you request his handling onto someone else. Please, just take this in for a second. You haven't seriously dated anyone since what's-his-face last season."

"Do not invoke his name, Jessica.. He appears like Beetle-juice and I don't have the mental capacity for it now."

"I know. But listen, he was horrible, and it's about time you had a guy who took care of you for once, you know? You two can compartmentalize this, and keep the personal separate from the professional, I know you can."

"This sounds like it could go bad, and what happens then?" I watch Elliot step away from the shoot, pulling the suit jacket down off of his broad shoulders. My mouth runs dry as I watch his back muscles flex beneath the white dress shirt.

"I don't know how to make this happen, Jess, the head office will skin us alive if it goes bad. I mean, a workplace scandal at this level is national news. I'm scared to lose everything."

"Maybe you will, maybe it will go down in flames. But what if it doesn't?"

"You are far too chipper about all of this." I bite on a hang-nail. "Okay fine. I still don't know what to do about it though!"

"Just let whatever happens, happen. Not everything in life requires an itinerary or a rulebook."

Elliot walks toward me, his eyes narrowing with a head tilt like he's asking, "everything okay?"

"I'll take it under advisement. Thanks, Jess. I'll see you when I get back."

"Have fun with your hockey boy! Earn some time in the Sin Bin!" Her bellowed statement is as loud as a speaker-phone. I try to cut off her loud statement as he approaches, hoping like hell he can't hear her. God, I could hear it like she was yelling right next to me.

I squeak as I try to hit the end button on my call, while I could hear Jess's maniacal laughter, even from a distance. I shoot a panicked look at Elliot, now standing in front of me, the right side of his mouth ticking upward and making that dimple pop in and out of his cheek.

"You heard that, didn't you?" I sigh as he bites his bottom lip, holding in an impish grin.

"Maybe. Are you about ready to get out of here? I'd love to go get something to eat with you, it's the least I can do after dragging you here."

"Yeah, sounds great, especially if you're buying." God, Ronni, that wasn't smooth at all! "I'm ready if you are."

"Awesome. Let's go." He starts to walk away from me, but then pauses. I can teach you how to earn some time in the Sin Bin, Snow Queen." He winks, and keeps walking away.

At that moment, I didn't know if I want to kill Jessica or give her a cake. I started following a chuckling Elliot, anyway.

"I don't know what you thought you heard, but it's not what you think."

"Your friend said to earn some time in the Sin Bin. You know who spends a lot of time there?"

"Duh, Mox, I know hockey slang. It's the penalty box, your home away from home."

"Right. And how do you get in the penalty box, Ronni?"

"You break the rules."

Elliot reaches in front of me, opening the door to the stairwell and holding it open so I can go in ahead of him and descend the stairs. I hear the door click closed behind him as I reach the next landing down, and look up to see if he's going to continue this line of questioning as we walk. He's down the stairs faster than I can think, his heat enveloping me as I press back against the wall.

"I think we're breaking a rule now." His voice, soft and gravelly, whispers past my ear as he moves closer, and closer still, to put his hands on the wall beside my head. My world narrows to the space between us. The dichotomy of the cool concrete against my back and his warm body pressed to the front of me made my head spin, and I shiver. I glance up into his face, his eyes laser focused on mine, and time stood still.

"Mox, I…we," I whisper back, my mind racing from one thought to the next. I was barely aware of my hands reaching up along his sides.

"Shh, I know." His lashes fluttered as his eyes closed, and his head lowered enough to rest his forehead against mine. "All I could think about for the last hour was how your lips felt against mine. How I wanted to do it again," he said as moved slightly to hover his lips over mine. "I wondered if you would let me do it again."

Time grinds to a halt. Nothing exists outside of here and now, and the light puffs of our breaths mingling in this tiny space between us.

"Why did you stop?" I whisper. I could feel him, so close to where he promised to be, yet so far away.

"You didn't say yes yet. It's killing me, Snow Queen, please say yes and put me out of my misery."

I say nothing with words, simply pressing forward and resting my lips against his. I could feel his growl vibrate against my lips and my heart racing against my chest. One hand moves off the wall, wrapping around the back of my neck to pull me closer still. My curls tangle around his thick fingers, making me gasp as his tug pulls on them.

"Jesus, don't tell me you like that," he groaned against my lips.

"Okay, I won't," I breathe.

His eyes turn glassy as he looks at me. "Somehow I don't believe you, but I don't care right now."

My eyes roll back a bit as the hand in my hair tightens, sliding my head to the left so he can attack the side of my neck with his lips.

"Mox, what are we…we shouldn't, the team…," I whisper as my head falls backward. My head is saying no, but my heart and body are saying hell yes, and I don't know how to put it together and make sense.

"Fuck the team. No. Don't do that. I'd have to fight them all."

A nervous laugh burst past my lips at his statement. Oh my God, what are we doing? "We're going to get caught," I whisper against his lips as he dives in again. I feel drunk and like I'm flying, but my limbs are heavy all at the same time.

A door opening in the stairwell scares a scream out of me, and I shove him hard in the chest. He put one finger against his lips and stands still, freezing. A steady "clip clip clip" of heels could be heard above us, so I walk down the flight of stairs in the direction we were heading initially. After a few steps, I notice that he's not behind me.

"Come on, let's go," I motion to him as I continue descending the stairs. He's standing still, eyes glazed and staring blankly at the wall before him. A shake of his head, and he trudges behind me.

"We're not done with this," he murmurs at me as we reach the bottom floor, before we enter the hallway to the lobby.

"Yeah, Mox, we are. We have to be at the moment."

"Don't make it stop before we ever start, we'll talk about this later."

I shoot him a look and stride across the lobby, weaving between people. I can't look back before he makes me second guess myself.

CHAPTER 14

ELLIOT

THERE'S a feeling that I thought I had totally gotten accustomed to early in my hockey career. It's like I've been electrified, I can feel my nerve endings spark and jump, ready to launch into motion at a moment's notice. Pre-game, it's normal. We're all hyped and ready to tear out onto the ice and everything feels pressurized. Like a spring pulled too tight, and about to launch.

This feeling is lodged in my chest now, as I sit in my penthouse and stare at my phone. I should call her, maybe apologize for earlier. I all but launched myself on her like a freaking animal, after all. I'm not really sorry, but it might smooth things over some. She's right, even if I don't agree totally.

HR would have a heyday I'm sure, if they found out the team captain's new hobby was fraternizing with the staff. It's not the first time a team has had relationships form between different levels of employees. The biggest difference now was I'm the team captain, the one that was supposed to lead by example, and she's the support staff. I'm pretty sure someone would take offense to the power imbalance here, but frankly I don't care. I want her in my life so badly that I'm about to say fuck the rules and go get my girl. That felt amazing to me; calling her my girl, even if it's only in my head.

But seriously, I like her. She's spunky, and she didn't let me get too serious about myself. I smile as I remember how she can take me down a notch with just a few well-placed jabs. Right when I thought I was the best of the best on ice, she gives me a verbal beat down I can't deny. And the most frustrating part of all of this is that she doesn't even know she worked her way under my damn skin. She's oblivious to the struggle it is to live up to her expectations occasionally. Worst of all—or maybe best of all—I feel the happiest trying to please her. I want her happiness more than the MVP title, or the Cup, or any other recognition anywhere.

I groan and throw my head back against the couch. *I should just call her, get this out of my system and be done with it,* I think to myself. If she gets me called into HR, so be it. If I don't get this out in the open, I might very well explode.

"Pull your shit together, Moxley," I grumble at myself as I reach forward for the phone. Before I could second guess myself, I dial her number. My heart dropped, thinking that she'd sent me to voicemail after the second ring, but she picked up.

"Hey, Moxley," she said, and I think I pick up the slightest bit of hesitation in her voice. I rarely call her, so I'm not totally surprised to hear it.

"Hey, Snow Queen. Um," I pause, trying to pull my thoughts together. "Are we okay? I just wanted to make sure you were okay after earlier."

"Oh, yeah, that." I could hear her move around and wonder what she's up to tonight. "Yeah, we're good. I mean, it was just a momentary lapse in judgment, no need to make it any bigger than it already is."

I sigh on my end. She had no idea, really. I ramp up my flirting game with her; I drop little compliments and suggestions in our regular conversations and she just continues on like I didn't just say anything. Is she oblivious to my charm? I mean, she had to be aware of it; she called me out on all my bullshit before when I'd been my usual self in public, but when it's directed at her, it goes nowhere. I want nothing more than to scream it from the rooftops but I just visualize her giving me that stern look over the top of her tablet and saying, "well, now that you have that out of your system, how about if we get back to work."

"Hey, Ronni?"

"That's Veronica to you, sir."

"I know. Um, so, what would you say if I said it wasn't just a lapse in judgment?"

"I'd say you need to go back to the team trainer about your concussion protocol. Clearly you rattled your little jock brain loose."

"I don't think so," I respond. "I think it's something we've been working toward for a while. You really don't know what I've been thinking about lately, do you?"

"The idea of you thinking of anything is scary sometimes, Moxley," she said with a chuckle. "Do I even want to ask what you have thought about?"

Well, this is it. Shoot your shot, big guy. She's either going to block the shot or you'll get a bar-downski celly, dude.

"I think," I pause for a breath, "that I've been trying to tell you I like you for a long freaking time, and it's fallen on deaf ears. I think I would like nothing more to meet your lofty standards that I keep falling short of every time I try. I think that you absolutely drive me crazy and I can't stop thinking about you to begin with."

"Moxley, you can't really mean any of that," she sighs.

"I think I'm tired of you putting yourself down every time I throw a sincere compliment to you. I also think that you're beautiful when you're ranting at me and I can't help but mess up just to watch you get fired up with me again." I could hear her protest. "Before you say anything against yourself, I think while you're beautiful when you tell me I'm wrong, you're positively radiant when you're fully invested in solving a problem and I think I'd love to find out what it feels like to have that passion and energy turned toward me."

"You can't be serious, I'm not that pretty…"

"No. Don't say it. Be respectful when you're talking about my girl." I hear her breath rush from her, and then silence. "Talk to me, pretty thing, I don't know what to do when you're quiet."

"I can't really be your girl…"

My heart clenches at her soft words. I can't let her continue that thought.

"Why not? What is stopping you?"

"You're you, obviously. You can get any girl you want and I'm, well, I'm just me. I'm no one important and I'm not your usual type."

"Reading up on my exploits, Ronni?" She huffs, and I know it's from the use of her nickname. Grinning, I double down on my determination to break that rule down at some point.

"That's not really what I meant. I mean, you've dated models and I'm not that. I'm the opposite of that."

"You're exactly what I want. I want someone who makes me think and work hard, not someone who knows how to play up the cameras."

"It's still not really allowed. I could get fired. You could be traded. ESPN would have a fresh scandal for ratings and, Mox, you're already on their radar. This wouldn't help."

"If none of the rules and regulations were in the way, what would you do? Would you let me date you? Could I spoil you, treat you like the queen you are?"

I hear my racing heartbeat against the phone. I need her answer like I need air. I need to know.

"Yes, I probably would." Her answer was so soft I almost miss it. I barely withhold my fist bump. He shoots, he scores.

"So if I can get rid of the rules, will you?"

"Will I do what?"

"If I can make sure you aren't penalized for this, will you see me? I gotta know."

"Okay." It was barely a whisper, and yet it echoed in my skull. Oh, my god. This was it.

"Okay?"

"Yeah, okay. I," she paused, "I think I would like that. But I'm scared, though. I love my job, I can't afford to lose it. And if you get traded…"

Her words trail off into a sigh, and I understand where she's coming from. There's a lot hanging in the balance on this. We both have a lot to lose if this goes bad, or if the organization had an issue with it.

"I know. And I don't want to make things hard for you. I just really, really want to see what's between us. There's something. I know you felt it too."

Her breath shuddered across the line and I smile.

"You're right. But, what are we going to do about it?"

"I have a few ideas. I think you might even like them."

"Oh, do you? Like what?" Her voice had a lilt to it I don't remember hearing before.

I freeze. Was she seriously interested or was she just entertaining me? "Um, well, first off, I'd need to actually take you on a proper date. Not a work function, not a planning meeting at a coffee shop. An honest to goodness date. I pick you up, we go to dinner, and we don't talk about work at all. Just a guy taking his girl out."

A giggle came across the line. "That sounds sweet. Where would we go?"

"I'm not giving away all of my secrets," I chuckle. "But a proper dinner, and then we'll go somewhere without ice."

"I should hope so; you spend enough time there as it is. So," she pauses and I can hear her shifting around, "is that a surprise too?"

"Of course. Do you trust me?"

"Maybe."

I nod to myself. "I'll have to work on that. I'll earn your trust, treat you like a lady, and prove that I'm not just a dumb jock with more money than sense."

Her sigh came across the line. "No one actually thinks you're a dumb jock, you know that, right? You've made some questionable decisions, but nothing actually malicious."

"I read, Snow Queen. I know what they've said about me on the blogs and the news segments. I'm getting better, but they still say it. I mean, you've even said it…"

"Oh, Elliot, I didn't really…you don't think I really meant it, do you?"

I bit my bottom lip, trying to keep the truth in. "Maybe early on you did? Anymore now it doesn't feel like you believe it like you did earlier in this thing."

"I've never thought you were an actual dumb jock. I mean, you're obviously a jock, but everything you've done has had a purpose behind it. Going to the club last month, I know you only did it to help RoJo. Clubbing the night before a game isn't your usual thing."

"I didn't tell you that, I don't think."

"I know you didn't. I found out from the boys."

"Sneaky bastards," I laughed, "should've known they'd run their mouths. What else did my teammates tell you about me?"

"I'm not giving away all of my secrets," she mimics my previous retort. "It's clear that they respect you and your choices, and they want to make sure you can stay."

I smile, thinking of how my team had my back. We truly were a cohesive unit and would go to war for each other.

"I'm glad they feel that way, because I really don't want to leave either." I glance at my phone, noting the time getting late. "What are you doing, Snow Queen?"

"I'm talking to you, obviously," she teases. "But you

should probably get to bed soon if you're going to be any good on ice tomorrow."

"I know, I'll get there in a moment. Just answer me one question first." I hear her murmur her agreement and grin. "If I didn't have a home game tomorrow, would you come over?"

Her laughter was my only answer for what felt like an eternity. "No, Moxley, I wouldn't. I'm your PR rep, not a puck bunny. Earn it."

"Challenge accepted."

"I'll hold you to it," she chirps back. "Good night, Mox."

"Good night, my Snow Queen."

CHAPTER 15

VERONICA

I JOLT awake when I hear my phone buzzing away merrily before it plunges off of my nightstand and drops to the carpet with a muted thud. Rolling over with a curse, I try to reach it and see what—or who—is interrupting the one day a week we have a late start.

"Of course," I mutter as I looked at the screen, where Moxley's name flashes. Answering it to stop the buzzing, I groan, "I take back that dumb jock comment. You're interrupting my sleep."

His deep chuckle sets off the butterflies in my stomach. "You don't really mean that, Ronni."

"It's Veronica to you, and. At this hour? Make that Ms. Snow. You're in big trouble, mister."

"I know, I'm calling you before coffee. But what if I told you I have something for you and I'm at your door right," he pauses, and I hear my doorbell, "now."

"No, you're fucking not. I'm not ready! What the hell, Moxley?" I hang up on him and fling myself out of bed with a groan, then race to the mirror to assess how bad I look this morning. My messy bun is falling loose, and I have on baggy yoga pants and a worn out t-shirt from one of last year's events. With a groan, I grab one of my oversized hoodies to throw over the top. I re-twist my bun as I walk to the door.

Peeking through the peephole, I groan as I realize he is totally put together, and holding a brown bag and a drink carrier.

I wrench the door open, giving him a look. "I come bearing gifts," he says cheerily, holding the treats out to me. I take the drink holder, and hold the door open to allow him in.

"Has anyone ever told you how ungodly chipper you are in the morning?"

"Yep, I room with Kozzy, he says it's stupid that I wake up like this. I thought you were more of a morning person than this."

"Poor Kozlov, he doesn't get paid enough for putting up with you. Did you forget the morning after the Sin Bin? That's morning. All the time."

"Oh, I thought that was just a hangover." He sits down on my loveseat, pulling small wrapped things from within the bag and arranging two place settings on the coffee table. "Come, sit down and eat. You need breakfast. Carbs and caffeine will make it all better."

"Have I entered the twilight zone? You're feeding me now?"

He looks up at me, his gaze serious. "You're horrible at taking care of yourself, and you almost always forget breakfast on game days because you're running around. So come, sit down and eat, and then we'll go to the arena so you can burn it off chasing us down for last-minute postings." He motions to the seat beside him. "Come on, it's getting cold."

I ease onto the seat, allowing him to take hold of the drinks while I get comfortable. He separates the drinks, putting one in front of each of us. Looking at the cups, I notice the difference in the marks. "What did you get?"

"Oh, I got your usual quad shot. I just went with an Americano." He points at the number 4 on the side of my cup. "I don't know how you manage with that on game day, but more power to you."

"It just does," I murmur, picking up the cup and breathing in the warmth. "I still can't believe you know these things."

"Jess filled me in."

I pause. "You've talked to Jess about me?"

"Well, yeah, I had to get into your good graces somehow. She said the way to your heart was with coffee. So, I brought coffee."

I smile at him. "She's right. Coffee helps."

He seems pleased that I like it, and I watch him visibly relax more.

"Well, get it in you, we all know it does you no good cold. And eat, so you can get ready to go," he scolds.

His mothering tugs on my heartstrings, and as I unwrap my bagel and take a bite, I think back on all the previous times he's stepped up to make sure I took care of myself. But then again, he didn't do it only to me. I've watched him take care of the young rookies coming in with a big brother kind of vibe that has been commented on in interviews. He really was sweet and caring and would be a great boyfriend, and husband or father someday.

I swallow heavily as that thought hits me.

Where did that come from? I mean, sure he's better than any other guy I've dated recently, but for my head to jump that far forward was a bit much! We just discussed yesterday!

Just enjoy your time, I told myself as I continued to chew under his watchful eye. This is only as serious as we want it to be, after all.

As I finished my bagel and gather my wrapper, he reaches over to me. "You have a little cream cheese right there," he murmurs as he slides his thumb along the corner of my mouth, gathering the bit of cream before pulling it away slightly.

I didn't even think before grabbing his thumb and licking

the white spot off. I feel us both freeze, our eyes locking on each other.

"Um," I stammer, his hand barely an inch in front of me, then pause, taking my bottom lip nervously in between my teeth.

His eyes slam shut, his face screwed up like he's in pain, before I feel him lower his hand out of mine, away from my face. With a sigh he mutters, "fuck it," and then he's back, closer than before, his lips crashing into mine.

If I thought the photo shoot was a once in a lifetime experience, I was wrong. How he made each encounter feel like the first time was beyond me, but I certainly would not complain about it. Stars explode behind my eyes as he held my head still and attacked.

I nibble on his bottom lip, smiling slightly at the growl that escaped him. With a slight twist, he has me up and deposited across his lap. A squeak escapes me as he moves me where he wants, his large hands anchoring my hips in place. I should panic, but I'm not. I'm the opposite, actually, and instead pushing for more. Spearing my hands into his hair, I pull his head back from mine. His eyes are closed, his breath escaping in short pants, and I just take it all in.

The sight of this man, normally so dominant on the ice, and he has handed over complete control to me. I dropped a soft kiss against his Adam's apple, chuckling slightly as it bobs under my touch.

"Jesus, you have no clue what you do to me," he whispers, his fingers flexing at my sides. I shift slightly over him, pleased at his sharp intake of breath. "I don't want to rush us, I want us to enjoy this, and—Fuck," he gritted out the curse as I rock again. "Babe, you're killing me, and damnit, I shouldn't before a game."

"You shouldn't? Why not?" I whisper into his ear, before tugging the lobe and hearing him curse again.

"There's, oh God, a theory that, shit, sex before a competition will–oh, shit, right there–hurt your performance. Fuck, Ronni, I need," with a groan he threw his head back against the couch while he rolls his hips slightly under me. "I usually don't play that great afterward, muscles are too loose, but I'll be damned if I don't want to see if you break the routine."

I pause, looking down at him, as I take in what he's saying. "So you don't...you know...on game days?"

He shakes his head vigorously, "Nope. Not even a little."

"Then we won't."

"Huh?"

His eyes shoot open, looking at me wildly.

"You're not going to mess up your game today. I won't be the reason your game is crap. There's time later."

Slowly, on shaky legs, I got up from his lap and headed toward my room, glancing back at him sitting shell shocked on my couch, I giggled before escaping behind the closed door. My heart still racing, I ran to my closet. I had to get ready, we had to leave before we threw caution to the wind.

CHAPTER 16

ELLIOT

MY HEAD IS SPINNING, my heart racing, and I don't know what just happened. One second, we're eating breakfast, being buddies, and then it's like we just spontaneously combust. Again. It's a recurring theme, and I don't know why I can't keep my focus with her.

Although, I think she's just as affected as me at this point. Her rapid escape said as much. I can still feel her lips against mine, her scent all around me.

What. The? Hell?

I told myself I wouldn't rush her, and I said that we needed to be careful until we knew what was going on for sure, but I'll be damned if I didn't want to just skip the game for her. There's no way I can get away with that, not with the way they're eyeballing me in the office, but damn I would do it if she asked. I only came by with breakfast so we could chill and talk before the game.

Sucking in a shaky breath, I smooth a hand down the front of my button down and straighten out my tie. Get yourself together, Moxley, I tell myself as I continue the box breathing I learned early in training. Slow breath in, pause, slow breath out. Focusing on the breathing made my thoughts slow a bit.

"So, um, about all that," Ronni's voice says behind me. I turn my head toward her, and see her leaning against the wall, her fingers twisting nervously in front of the Ice Wolves jersey she wore.

"No, no way. Who?" The words came out sharper, rougher than I intended.

"Uh…what?"

"Who's jersey is that?"

"Oh," she looks down. "It's…well, it's mine. We were all given jerseys in the grad internship program." She takes a step closer and turns so I can see the "Snow" on her back with the "13" in block numbers.

I nod my head in approval, but I'm berating myself. Quit acting like a freaking animal!

"That was nice of them."

"Whose jersey did you think I was wearing?" I scowl a bit and shrug.

"I don't know. Maybe Koz, or Bishop, someone established with a long contract. And single."

She looks at me, her brow furrowed in confusion, before realization dawns on her face. "You're jealous I'm not wearing yours."

My head shakes firmly before the words can even form. "Not that, but…if you're going to wear a player jersey, I'll get you mine first."

Her chuckle makes me feel a little embarrassed about what I've said. I narrow my gaze, and her chuckle grows into a full-blown laugh. I close my eyes and wonder just how stupid I look now that I've started down this path.

"Aw, don't take it personally. I wouldn't wear anyone's jersey unless I had to, anyway. It's going to have to be someone or something super important that makes me wear an active player's jersey."

Ouch. That hurt. I felt the little bubble of pride at seeing her in my jersey again shrivel and die. I still had some work to do with her. At least I had that one moment early in the season, even if it was an accident.

"That's fine. That's totally cool," I grumble, sitting up. "So, if you're ready we can go to the arena now. Unless you had something else you needed to do first." I move to get off of the sofa and gather the breakfast things. "I just thought that you'd like to have a ride, and I know you get in early."

"No one will think we're up to something if we show up together, right?"

I look up to Ronni, where she's standing by the desk, fussing with her backpack straps. She's biting that bottom lip of hers again, but I get what she's telling me.

"No, why would they? Occasionally the boys carpool together. It's just two coworkers carpooling, I think. Are you worried? I can meet you there. I probably should've just done that. I'm sorry. I should have thought about this."

"No, it's cool, I just didn't want you to get in trouble if I'm getting out of your car. But you're right, I mean, we've been at how many events together now? Sorry, I'm just over-thinking."

"Ronni." Her eyes shoot up at me, but she doesn't give me her usual line about calling her Veronica. "It's okay. If you aren't comfortable, we won't. Don't make yourself uncomfortable. And stop apologizing so much."

"You're right, sorry. I mean, shit...sorry. Damn it!" She chuckles. "Let's go so you can primp pre-game. Rumor has it that Jess has her intern doing entrance videos for social media today, and I know what the pop quiz question is this time."

I pause, holding the door open for her as we walk out. "So, do I get to know?" We keep walking, and I wait for her answer. "No, really, what are they asking? I don't want to have a dumb answer." She smiles and slides her fingers across her lips in the universal "my lips are sealed" motion. "Oh, you're so evil," I chuckle, and opened the passenger side door for her. She slips her bag off of her shoulder and I take the weight from her hands. "I'll throw this in the back for you."

"Thanks, Mox. And they say that chivalry is dead."

"No, Ma would cuff the shit out of my head if she knew I wasn't holding doors and being a gentleman."

"It's adorable that she put all that effort into making you a gentleman, only for you to be the bad boy on a professional hockey team," she remarks as she slides into the passenger seat, and I softly shut the door between us. Clicking the remote in my pocket, I sat her bag down in the trunk, and then climb into the driver's seat beside her.

"You've never seen me at my full 'gentlemanly behavior' level, and I can prove it to you." I look at her, and wait for her to make eye contact with me. "If I wasn't a gentleman, I'd tell you what all I'd rather go back inside and do instead of playing hockey today."

Her eyes go wide, but neither one of us looks away. "So I suppose that means we should really head to the arena then," she whispered, blinking.

"Absolutely," I mutter, pulling out of the parking spot before I can change my mind.

CHAPTER 17

VERONICA

I DROP BONELESSLY into my chair and mull over what has gone on in the last few days. Apparently we're dating now, and that's just blowing my mind. I don't look like anyone that he's ever been with, at least on his social media. He'd always been with tall blonde models and I'm short, average, and just not magazine ready.

What are we doing? I can't wrap my head around this. And how did I go from hating his presence to, well…whatever this is.

"Girl, how's it going? Are you ready to come down to the locker room for entrances?"

I jumped and turned toward Jess, who is giving me a bemused look. "You scared the crap out of me! I'm ready if you are. Did you lose your intern?"

"Sort of. She's multi-tasking for me. But come on, we can go together and get entry shots! I'm really looking forward to getting Moxley's."

"He's already here," I respond and then curse when she whips her head back to look at me.

"How do you know that he's already here, Veronica?"

"Um," I pause, "he drove me here." Her side eye told me

to keep elaborating. "He stopped by to see if I wanted a ride in so I didn't have to fight with the parking."

"Uh, huh? And?"

"And nothing." More side eye. "Okay, he brought me breakfast." Head tilt. "We ate it. Together. In the living room, I swear." A stare over the top of her glasses. "Okay fine! We might have kissed."

"And?"

"And that was all because," I slam my lips together to keep the words in. "You know, it really isn't fair that you know I can't lie and that I can't *not* tell you anything. Government secrets are not safe here."

"I know all that. Now what I want to know is what you two are planning on doing about all this."

"I told you last night. He wants to date properly but we have to be careful. HR won't think too highly of him fraternizing with the help."

We continue to walk down the hall together, talking about the upcoming ball and the social media campaigns that she was preparing. The Foundation ball was the biggest event of the season and was the biggest stressor on our plates.

"You know, Ronni, I don't think they'd care. If anything, they might actually approve because you'd know better than to get him into trouble."

"I know, but I don't know how they'd feel with one of their top players and a PR person being a couple. I worry about that part of it."

"It's not like he's part of your management. He has no pull on our side. I think you'd be safe. There has to be some way for you two to stay together. You've been good to him, and for him, I think."

"I know. He's really not that bad of a guy, and he's been so easy to be around. I," I pause as we approach and pass an open doorway for the equipment managers, "I enjoy our time together. He's really a great guy, so funny, and I just want to see where we turn out."

"Well, keep at it. If it gets super serious, maybe then approach Michael and HR."

"I will," I promise. "It is really new, and not worth making waves yet."

"Exactly! When you guys make things serious, then you can discuss things. Until then, it's just fun."

"You're so right. I'm getting worked up for nothing." I smile. "Besides, it may go nowhere. He's him, and I'm me."

"What is that supposed to mean?" She asks with a frown. "You're beautiful and totally worthy of him! Just because he has a jawline for days that we use regularly for promo prints does not mean he's better!"

I glance sideways at her in disbelief. "He's dated actual freaking models before. I'm not that."

"You're awesome and he should be so honored to hang out with you," Jess retorts back. "Don't downplay yourself."

"I know." I shake my head, stuffing mini-mics into my backpack. "Anyway, we gotta go."

Before she can argue with me longer, I head off toward the locker rooms, and try to forget everything that has happened today. I need to focus on my job, and not what it felt like to be the center of Elliot Moxley's world for a minute.

CHAPTER 18

ELLIOT

GETTING ready for a game is a ritual. The socks go on the same, left sock then right. I wrap the tape exactly the same way every single time. I'm not as bad as some guys, I don't wear the same pair of socks for all the road games or anything gross like that. It's just repetition, step by step. If I do the things in order, my game is on point. It's been like that since I played in mites, and I refuse to change up at this point. However, I am pulling the tape off for the third time because I'll be damned if I can't fucking concentrate and it's wrinkled. Fucking rookie move I swear.

"Mox, you good?" Val Bishop sits across from me, tying his skate laces. I can feel him looking at me, and it does nothing to relax my nerves. He has twice the seasons under his belt that I do. His leadership is everything to me, ever since I was the young upstart with the captain's C on my chest. He's never been bitter about it, but he has that strong leadership energy that I wish I had. Feeling him pick apart my shortcomings this afternoon really does jack for me.

"I will be in a minute. This tape freaking sucks," I grumble at him, tossing another tape ball toward the trash can.

"Here, use this," he says, throwing me his roll of tape. I

nod my head in thanks at him and start concentrating on wrapping it around my shins again. Deep down, I know there was no difference between the two rolls. Hell, they probably came from the same box in the trainers' office this morning. Still, with the fresh roll, I complete the pattern I always use and then toss the roll back at him so I could focus on the skates next. One step at a time, one piece of gear at a time, and then I'll be ready. I wasn't just Elliot Moxley, dumb jock from the peewee leagues. I'm Elliot Fucking Moxley, Captain of the Ice Wolves, top scorer in the division, and…

I lose my train of thought as I look over and see Coach standing with Jessica and Ronni. She's in my locker room and I couldn't look away. I just saw her a couple hours ago, but for some reason I had forgotten what she looked like standing there in our colors. I grit my teeth as once again I see her in that jersey, and wish I could put her back in mine again. *Later, you Neanderthal,* I grumble inwardly as I continue putting my gear on.

"Alright, boys, look sharp!" As a unit, we all look toward Coach and fall silent. "Thank you for answering the social media questions on the way in the building. Now, on your way out for warmups, please catch up with Jess and Ronni, as they're getting more hype materials. They will be in the tunnel and filming the walk up, so please be aware of what you're doing and saying, okay? Good! Get back at it!"

He exchanges handshakes with both women—and I withheld a growl as I watch Ronni's face light up as she also clasps his wrist—before they both head toward the door. I keep my eyes trained on her, looking at that "Snow" in big white letters across her shoulder blades, and catch her eyes as she looks straight at me. I flash a wink at her, and grin as her cheeks go scarlet.

"Moxley." Bishop calls to me, drawing my attention away from Ronni's retreating back and over to him. "Come on, let's go chat."

Shit.

I follow him around the corner and into one of the therapy rooms. I hope my walk is nonchalant, but I have my doubts about that.

"Would you like to explain what that was?" He keeps his tone low, but I know that is for my benefit. The walls have ears in here sometimes.

"It's…. I don't know."

"What do you mean, you don't know? You're looking at the PR team a little intensely for you to not know what's going on."

"I mean I don't know what Ronni and I are doing yet. I asked her out, we're going to try dating, but we're keeping it quiet for now."

"You're dating from within the franchise. You know what will happen if word gets out, right?"

"I know, I know, I just…I like her. She doesn't have that hero worship thing with me, and I like I can just be myself when I talk to her. She sees it too."

"Are you going to play with your head in the game? You're going to see her all over the place. And is she why you were taping like you were in pee wee's again?"

"Don't start on me, Bish, that's just a one-time thing." He looks at me askance and I just smirk back. "I got a handle on this, and I can keep my head in the game. I mean it."

"If you say so. Let's go do this thing."

We fist bump and then head out into the locker room to see everyone else getting pumped up. The music is thumping through the overhead speakers and I feel myself get pulled into the frenetic movements of my teammates. This is the energy and distraction that I need to get through the day.

"Come on boys, let's show the Raptors how we do this! Skate hard, shoot smart. Eyes up. We've got this! Let's go let's go let's go!"

I delivered fist bumps and helmet taps to each player as they headed out the door, with Val bringing up the rear.

"Good job, Cap," he said to me as he double taps my fists.

I follow along behind him, out toward the tunnel. I could hear the crowd above us already, and it made me jittery. Arena workers and special guests line the sides of the hallway, waiting for fist bumps from us as we made our way to the ice. Around one corner, I see Jess and Ronni asking questions and filming our answers. I just barely catch the question being asked of all of us, our favorite ice cream. Oh, this is going to be so fun to answer.

Jess is tied up with Val's drawn out answer because he can't just pick one, which meant Ronni would get to ask me. Perfect. As I approach, she bites her lip a bit as she sees me coming, and shakes her head behind the phone she held.

"Hey, Moxley, what's your favorite ice cream?"

"Easy. A little Death by Chocolate with whipped cream and hot fudge on top. Maybe a cherry on top if I have one. Everything's better with whipped cream, though." I finish it with a wink.

I watch her put her phone down, tapping the screen to stop the recording, before she looks up at me with wide eyes.

"Well, that's one that can't make it onto social media."

"Why not?"

"That had a certain tone to it and you know it."

"Want me to do it again and say I prefer vanilla? No whipped cream?"

Her withering gaze should have made me feel sorry for jabbing at her, but I don't. I give her a little grin, and then cheered inwardly when she smiles back at me.

"So, I should keep Death by Chocolate in the freezer then?"

I leaned in close, so only she could hear me. "There won't be time for the ice cream, babe. However, the whipped cream has potential." Her gasp is audible, and I point toward the equipment hallway. "Got a sec?"

"Sure," she whispers, heading that direction. I follow her to the door, pulling it open before ushering her into the dark. "Aren't you supposed to be heading out for warmups?"

"I am, in a minute," I say, letting the door shut behind me and enveloping us in darkness. I reach out with my bare hand, keeping the other hand with my stick and gloves far away, and pull her as close to me as my gear would get her. "I needed to see you first."

Even in the dark, our aim is impeccable. Her lips land on mine and her arms wrapped around my neck, holding me close. She meets me, move for move, and it's electrifying. I. let my free hand slide down her back, holding her against me.

"You need to go warm up, you dork," she laughs, her lips pulling just off of mine. Her breath skates across my parted lips as I lean in for more, but she places her finger against them.

"Go. We can talk after the game."

In all the time I've played hockey, I have never wanted a game to end so quickly in my life.

CHAPTER 19

VERONICA

I WON'T LIE; I fully expected to find the whole team, coaches, someone outside the door when we left. There was no way we wouldn't get caught. However, I think that just amped up the entire scenario, the risk of getting caught. Good heavens, the things that man could do and get away with around here.

I sneak up the tunnel to stand by Jessica, who had already moved toward the bench to watch the warmups and gather more footage. The footage I was supposed to be helping with. Guilt churns in my stomach with the butterflies from Elliot's sneak attack, and I try to breathe them all away.

"You good, Ronni?" She's looking at me with her excited "game day" face on, but her eyebrows were dipping with obvious concern for me.

"Yeah, I'm good."

"Cool. Did you know your lipstick is smeared up your cheek?"

I smack my hand over my face and curse, flipping my phone's camera to selfie mode so I could look. She isn't wrong, there's a wine colored stain on my cheek, and what's worse, it's not on my lips hardly at all. Which means....

"That color does nothing for Moxley's skin tone," she chuckled at her own joke.

Damnit.

I look on, horrified, as Elliot skates by me and I can see that he's definitely looking a little off-color around his mouth as well.

"Shit-shit-shit," I grumble as I tried to wipe off my own stain. "He doesn't know, does he?"

"Don't think so, girl, or else he's absolutely cool with wearing it." I watch him skate around, volleying a puck back and forth with another player. He laughs at something they said, and grins toward me. Shaking my head at him, I look over at Jessica, who is busting a gut looking between us. "It's okay, I mean, what's the worst that'll happen? You two are cute together."

"And fraternizing."

"And you're still cute."

"That won't mean anything to HR."

"Don't be so negative about it. It'll be okay."

We watch him skate toward us, flashing me a wink as he approaches the bench.

"Hey, Mox," I shout over the crowd, and he skids to a halt in front of me.

"Hey, Snow Queen," he replies, smiling at me.

"Come here," I motioned him forward until his thick, black gloves are on the rail on either side of mine, and then lean forward so I can speak into his ear. "Do you know you're wearing more of my lipstick than me?"

He pulls back to look me in the face. "I know, Robey told me about it. It looks good on me, eh?" He bites his bottom lip mischievously as he skates backward, away from me. "See ya later!" With a wink, he skated off, offering fist bumps to his teammates as he goes.

"I'm in so much trouble," I mutter, watching him drop to

the ice and stretch his lower body with Robicheaux and Bishop.

"Yeah, girl, you are," Jess chuckles at me and I just lower my head.

I continue to look over the ice and gather photos of the team as they proceed with warmups. The energy feeling really good from the team, and the crowd is still roaring. This has the makings of a great matchup and should work really well for the media teams.

Quickly, the players started filing back to the locker room so the Zamboni can clean the ice. As Elliot walks past me, winking, and I try to avoid eye contact with him as he laughs, and I hear Duffy rib him as he walks away.

"This is impossible. Do you need help going through the footage for the posts? I can head back to the office now and get a head start, you don't really need me over here, right?"

She shoots me a look that said I'm not getting out of this. "If I'm here, you're here. Don't leave me alone!" Her head shook viciously. "Definitely don't leave me alone around here with these guys."

I followed her down the tunnel and looked closely at her. She definitely seemed off her game and looks...shaken. "Are you okay? Did someone do something?"

"No, it's not that. Or, not anything I didn't consent to." She pauses, looking to the left and right before sending me down a side hall. "So, I may have had a slight interaction with Bishop."

"By interaction you mean..."

She sighed at me, and I looked down. "I ran into him at the club and things...happened. We said we'd talk about it afterward but it hasn't really materialized yet. He's also so headstrong and, well, such a freaking Dom..."

"Wait. You mean that club?" Her eyebrow lifts at me. Of course she meant that club. I knew she had planed to meet Roby there, but I didn't know Bishop visited as well. "He can't have that going on the record anywhere. Head office will have a fit. I mean, if you two are happy with it, cool, but they don't see it the same way."

"I know. That's why we were planning on talking about it. Instead, he gets all shitty if I'm doing my job and just barely touch someone else."

"Go talk to him after the game. You two really need to hash this out."

"We'll get there. Come on, let's go. We have a game to track and being hot messes won't get us anywhere."

Together we head to the side office and upload the videos we've gathered, so she can prep the posts for the period. We keep the conversation light, laughing about the answers given on some of them. We get to Elliot's and she just rolls with laughter.

"That guy, I swear. I know he rubs you wrong most days, but he's great for entertainment value."

"I know, there's never a dull moment there. He's not horrible to hang out with off the clock, either."

"That's good, since you're practically dating now."

I shush her, looking around to make sure no one else could hear. "Dude, not cool!"

"Oh please, as if anyone would care. You might actually be good for his image, if you think about it. You aren't a party girl, you follow the rules, and you have a squeaky clean internet image."

"For now," I grumble. "I have doubts about his past not coming back."

Jess looks over at me. "You really think she'd come back?"

I shrug, and look down at the video I'm uploading to the Ice Wolves social media cloud from my phone.

"Who knows what she would do. No one expected her to do anything she did in the off-season, but look at what happened. She not only shook down his career but also nearly sabotaged her own. Calculation and strategy isn't really her jam, you know?"

"True. Has there been anything coming from her camp that you know of?"

"No. I'm just being cautious, I think."

The game continues around us, and I allow my thoughts to wander a bit. Would the silence mean anything? Would she actually come back around to cause more trouble? Things had fallen silent shortly after the initial bomb drop, for no apparent reason. The dying furor over her interview's reach had given us an opportunity to turn the media coverage around for him, but would she actually stay away, or would she try to come back?

CHAPTER 20

ELLIOT

I PLAYED the hardest game I've played in ages. Every time I thought I had everything under control, I would see her. Behind the bench, in the tunnel, even standing right outside the locker room. I couldn't get—or keep—my mind clear no matter how hard I tried. We still got the win, though, but it was ugly. Standing under the warm spray of the shower didn't help my feelings, though, and I just really need to get my shit together before I look like a stupid golden retriever puppy when I see her again.

I'm Elliot Mother-fucking Moxley, captain of the Ice Wolves, top scorer in the league, all-around great guy who gets everything he wants…and all I want is *her*. I want her to acknowledge me without that judgmental look in her eye, and maybe even say that I haven't been a total fuckup this season. I've gotten better. I've met every goal she set for me. I even went to the children's hospital dressed as Santa and I did it gratefully.

I smack the shower taps and turn off the water, wrap a towel around my waist and head to my locker. I usually go to Sami's and visit with Gabby after the game, but I'd like to see if Ronni will come with me. She knows about Gabby, and Gabby knows about Ronni, but they haven't met yet. I feel like this is a huge step for me, for us. By introducing her to my family unit, I'm letting her in. I've never officially introduced anyone to my family before. Sure, a couple fans stalked me to the hospital or to dinner with Sami, but I've never willingly made that step.

I listen to the rumblings of my teammates as they work their way out the door in their suits; the silence descending on the locker room as the crowd dissipates. I throw a few waves and fist bumps at the guys as they leave and I continue to get dressed.

"You good, Mox? You seem distracted tonight." Bishop is sitting on the bench beside me, and I have no idea how long he'd been there.

"Yeah, I'm good. I'm just tired. Ready to head home, I think. You?"

"In a minute. I wanted to talk to you first, and then I have something to wrap up with PR. Are you sure you know what you're doing? I mean, by chasing Ronni."

"I hope so. I just know I'm different when I'm with her. I like what she makes me try to be." He nodded at me, his forehead wrinkled in thought. He stayed quiet, and I let the silence hang between us.

"So, this isn't just another Lacey type situation, right? You aren't just trying to fill a gap in your life, or whatever it was that kept you attached to her for far too long?"

"Absolutely not, and Ronni isn't like her at all. I should've seen the red flags coming from a mile away, but I didn't. I really should've listened to everyone sooner about her and then I wouldn't have found myself in this position at all. Maybe I would've still been a fuckup, but maybe I would have skipped that whole thing altogether."

"Sounds like you're finally growing up, kid." He smiles at

me, then gets up off of the bench. "By the way, your girl is outside waiting on you."

"What the fuck, Bishop!" I growl at him as I hurry and throw clothes on. "Damnit, she probably thinks I'm dicking off in here!"

His laugh echoes off the walls of the empty locker room as I run out the door, nearly running into Ronni as I skid into the hall. She's leaning against the wall outside the doorway, face in her phone. She looks up into my face and smiles.

"Hi," I say breathlessly, grinning back at her smile.

"Hey," she answered softly. "I didn't know if you had your phone on you yet, and you said we would talk after the game, and you were my ride in earlier..." she trails off. "I'm babbling, sorry. Anyway, um, did you still want to talk?"

"Yeah. Let me grab my keys and we can head. Pick up dinner or something."

I try desperately to sound nonchalant about it, but I can hear my own nerves. *Get it together, Moxley.* She nods and grins wider at me.

"Sounds great. See you in the parking lot?"

"Nah, just wait. I'll be right out. Stay here."

I run into the locker room again, make a beeline to my locker and snag my phone, wallet, and keys. With a small nod at Bishop, I sprint back out the door. I have plans for the night. I throw a short text to Sami to let her know not to wait for me, and head out for the night.

Ronni is still leaning against the cinderblock wall by the door where I had left her earlier. Grinning, I grab her hand and start walking briskly around to the player entrance.

"Woah, slow down, my legs aren't that long," she laughs around the words as she breaks into a jog, trying to keep up with my longer strides.

"Nope, I'm not slowing down for anything!" With that, I bend down and throw her over my shoulder.

Hysterical laughter echoes off the walls as I keep up my pace.

"Jesus, Moxley, put me down, I can walk on my own!" Her hands are everywhere, pressing onto my back so she can lift her head up, smacking my butt, and all I could do is laugh at her. "Oh, you're so gonna get it when I get down!"

"Oh yeah? What am I gonna get when I put you down?"

My right forearm holds her thighs down against my chest, but my left is free to wander a bit. I slide my hand up the back of her thigh as I feel her smack on my back pocket again. "Better watch what you do with those hands, Snow Queen, I'll give as good as I get."

"Someone is going to see us," she hisses, landing another well-timed smack against my right asscheek.

"Someone is going to hear us first if you keep it up," I retort, returning the tap against her own, leaving my hand there. "Hold on tight." I sidestep into a hallway, dipping into an abandoned office and letting the door click shut behind us. I slide her body down the front of me in the dark, reveling in the feel of her touching me. She steadies herself, and I grab the sides of her head, holding her still as I kiss her soundly.

"What are we doing here?" She whisper against my lips in between kisses.

"Needed you, couldn't wait," I growl against her lips as I press her against the door, feeling her arms wrap around my neck.

"We need to go home, Mox, take me home, please," she begs, raking her fingers through my damp hair.

Fucking hell, this woman will be the death of me and I would go gladly into Valhalla for her.

"We will, promise, just one moment," I murmur, tasting her lips just one more time.

"'Kay," she sighs, relaxing into my touch more, pressing her own kisses along my jaw and my neckline, twisting her fingers in my tie as she did.

"Never getting enough of you, Snow Queen," I groan as she nips at my neck. "Okay, we need to go. Now."

With strength I didn't know I had, I step back from her, letting our breaths slow, and take her hand.

The walk to the parking garage felt like miles, but as we get there, and I hold the door for her, I know that this is what I've wanted in my life.

CHAPTER 21

VERONICA

I'VE NEVER SEEN anyone drive as fast as Elliot on the way back to his place. It was, after all, closer to the arena than mine. Clearly, he wasn't willing to wait the extra time to get across the city.

He played it cool across the lobby and until the elevator doors closed on us, before launching on me. His hands pulling me close and then they were just everywhere. One hand worked my ponytail holder loose while the other dove under the back of my jersey, callous-roughened fingertips dancing up my spine. His lips were firm and warm, his tongue dipped out to dance on the seam of my lips as he pressed my back against the wall.

"Too fucking long," he murmurs against my lips.

I pull my head back for a breath and to look at the floor indicator.

"Mox, you didn't push the button. We're not moving."

He pauses, looking over with a dazed expression. Cursing loudly, he smacks the button for his floor before focusing his attention back on me. He runs kisses down my jaw, all while his hands keep up a steady movement. The hand on the back of head follows the same dizzying path, slowly up and through my loose hair, then down between my shoulder blades, pressing me closer to his chest, while his other hand trailed along my spine and down, fingertips dipping just beneath the waistband of my jeans.

After what feels like an eternity, the elevator slowed to a halt, and the doors began to slide open. Grasping my hand, he pulls me quickly out of the elevator and down the hall. My heart pounding furiously reminds me of one thing: this was actually going to happen.

With a quick movement, he unlocks the door, shoves us inside, and then slams the door shut behind us. In a move eerily similar to earlier at the arena, he gathers me up and hauls me toward the back of his apartment, tossing me on the bed in a tangle of limbs before prowling onto the mattress with me.

"Be gentle," I whisper, as I slide backward until my hands touch the pillows.

"As you wish," he replies with a grin, sliding his hand up my leg. "Tell me what you like, I want to hear you say it." The hand continues moving upward, taking my jersey with it. "The louder the better."

"O-okay," I stutter as that single hand slid higher still, joined by the other sliding the jersey off, leaving me in just my bra. He leans back, looking at me laying there. A large palm trailed down my stomach to the waistband of my pants, quickly unbuttoning them and then peeling them down my legs.

"You're fucking gorgeous like this." Without another moment of hesitation, he launches, laying across me, kissing me deeply again and then sliding his mouth down my neck. I couldn't breathe, and I just can't spend another moment not feeling him. I grasp against anything, just to hold him closer for a moment.

He continues his downward movement, trailing kisses along my overheated skin. His large hands are on my hips, holding me down against the bed as I move helplessly under his touch. I feel more than I hear his growl as he nips at my hipbones, his gaze up at my face.

"El, what are you, oh!" I gasp as he slid a hand up the inside of my thigh, pressing it out and away.

"Are you still with me?" His firm grasp doesn't waver, the steady pressure grounding me to the bed. My heart jumps in my chest as my brain fog clears just enough to realize he's still checking in for consent. I nod, and he lowers his head, dropping a soft kiss against my leg before launching a full-blown attack against me.

There were no words, just a continuous sensation.

The man is as skilled here as he is on the ice. Precise movements, soft touches. My eyes rolled back in my head as he performed a wicked assault with his tongue against my clit while twisting his fingers inside me.

"Oh, God." I moan on a sharp exhale, my hands at his sides moving up to grasp his shower dampened hair.

"Nope, not God. Just me." Before I get my wits about me, he's on the move again. His hands digging into the nightstand, pulling out a foil packet before I could ask what he was doing. With a wink he puts on the condom before sliding between my thighs again. "Are you ready?"

"Yes," I whispered on a breath, watching him slowly, carefully lining himself up. This had the potential to hurt tomorrow. So slowly, so carefully, he eases himself in, clearly allowing myself to adjust to his size. With a slide of my legs around his hips, I pulled him closer.

"Fucking hell, Ronni," he curses as he slides all the way in. I gasp, the pleasure-pain shocking me in a way I didn't anticipate. "Did I hurt you?"

"No, I'm good. Keep going."

He shifts his hips, the small movement pressing his pubic bone directly against my over-sensitized clit. I moan, grasping at his shoulders, scoring my nails across the skin there. I watch in awe as his eyes roll back at the action, and then he backs out just to press forward again. He lowers himself to his elbows, keeping up the slow grind as he presses kisses against my throat.

"Fuck, babe, you're killing me, so damn tight, so good," he murmurs against my skin, the words of praise rumbling through me. I feel a hand slide under the small of my back, and another into the back of my hair. Without a word he hoists me up, straddling his thighs as he continues rocking me against him. "That's my girl, take it," he growls as I adjust to the new position, and keep up the motion myself. He slides a hand between the two of us, his thumb strumming my clit. I can feel the orgasm building in me. "Are you going to come? Do it, come all over me, shit, I'm not going to last long like this, fuck." His dirty babble continues as I begin to flutter around him, and then he roars, arching his head back and pressing me harder, against him. Our heavy breaths echo in the room as we come down from our highs.

"That was—"

"Yeah. It was." His lips press to mine for a moment before he lowers us both to the mattress, pulling the comforter up and around us, without breaking us apart. Soft, gentle nips grow impatient before he trails them down my neck again.

Oh God, he's not done, I think deliriously as he continues his assault. Apparently he didn't need a lot of time to bounce back. If I make it through the night, someone needs to build a statue in his honor.

CHAPTER 22

WAKING UP SLOWLY, I look over, and my world grinds to a halt. Ronni is in my bed.

Veronica Snow is in. My. Bed.

Oh, my God. It's like my birthday, Christmas, and every trophy I ever wanted all rolled into one. I had no words for what that feels like. Her hair is spread wildly across my dark pillowcase, my sheets are tucked in a wrinkled mess under her arm. One foot hangs out of the covers and dangles off the edge of the mattress.

My heart races my breaths quick as I realize that this isn't just a really hot dream. No, she is definitely in my bed, pulling my arms around her further as she presses back into me. This might kill me but I'd die happy at this point.

"Good morning," I whisper in her ear, pressing a kiss just below her lobe. She arches back into me more, just like I hoped she would, and then slides a hand up my thigh.

"Morning. What time is it?" Her voice is low and gravelly with sleep, which apparently I like a lot as I feel myself twitch at the small of her back. God, she's trouble.

"We have plenty of time before we need to head to the arena. No need to get up yet."

She hums happily and does that roll with her hips again. "Cool. I have plans for you."

Fucking hell, I think to myself as I bit my lip against the groan that tried to escape me. I'm going to die. I'm going to die and I'll be happy about it.

"What plans are those?"

"Oh, just something I thought of, and you might like." She shifts in my hold and presses me to my back, before straddling my hips lightly.

"Keep talking. God, you look so fucking good up there." She giggles as she rocked, the sensation making my eyes roll back in my head. "Don't stop."

"Wasn't planning on it. But this wasn't it," she said, lowering herself to plant kisses across my pecs. And then shifted lower still.

"No? What were you–oh, fuck, Ronni!" Breath whooshed out of me as she wrapped her lips around me. I slam my eyes shut, I don't dare look down at what she's doing before I completely embarrass myself. "Shit, baby, that's, oh God–"

Nirvana. Heaven. Valhalla. I don't even know where I am anymore. I'm lost in her. My hands dive into her hair, holding her hair back so I can watch her work.

Gorgeous. She's so damn beautiful.

She tortures me for an eternity, pulling me so close to the edge just to slow me down with soft kisses, and then ramp me back up again, just to repeat the process.

This is the end. I'm sure of it.

With a herculean effort, I pull her back up, pressing her down onto the mattress with my larger size, grinding against her, leaving us both breathless.

"Elliot, please." Her hands slide up my pecs as I sit back, throwing her calf over my arm.

"Please what? Tell me what you want, I need to hear you." I dropped a kiss on her shin as I started rocking against her again. Her hands cover her face and I hear her mumble something behind them. "Can't hear you, sweetheart, tell me how you want me. I know you can. Do you want me here," I asked as I slid my head against her.

"Please," she begs, her back arching as she did.

As much as I want to draw this out, I just couldn't. With a small shift, I slid myself home, my groan and her gasp music to my ears. Each move ratcheted me up just that much higher. Would I ever get enough of her? I doubted it. I am thoroughly addicted to this.

Her breath hitched on a deep upstroke, and I feel her flutter. I can't hang, I feel my pleasure tightening like a spring, and I can do nothing except ride the waves out.

"That's my girl, so good." My breath hissing between my teeth as I try to keep up the rhythm she likes. With one last moan from her I'm helpless to hang on. Stars erupt behind my eyelids as I groan with my release. This is my everything. Leaning down to press kisses against her neck again, I swore I found my forever.

"This is going to be a bitch to hide at work," she murmurs sleepily as she curls into my warm body again.

"It's fine, I don't think anyone would care." I'm determined, I won't let anyone mess with this. "We're perfect together. No one can mess with us."

"I hope you're right. I want to stay like this forever." I smile at her breathy confession.

"Me too, Snow Queen. Me too."

I WOKE up with a giant heat rock against my back, and my limbs held down by the apparent tentacles of Elliot "I'm a cuddly octopus" Moxley. I need to get up and I can't untangle myself no matter how hard I try.

"I didn't say you could get up," he murmurs against my ear as he throws a calf over mine, pulling me back into him tighter.

"Mox, I need to pee, let me go," I giggle as I try to extricate myself again. With a groan, he lets go, and I scramble out from under the covers to run toward his bathroom.

"You're coming back when you're done, I'm not finished with you yet!" His yell penetrates the door with a chuckle.

I finish and wash my hands, attempting to smooth out my ruffled hair and cool the flush in my reddened cheeks. I look like a mess, but I can't take the smile off of my face. Who is this girl, I think to myself as I open the door and nearly walk into Elliot leaning on the door frame.

"Shit, you scared me," I said breathlessly, stepping back.

"I missed you."

"Apparently," I chuckle before stepping closer. "We don't have much time before we have to go back to work, do we?"

He shook his head no, telling me what I knew deep down. I popped up on my toes, dropped a kiss against his mouth, and edged around him into the dimly lit bedroom. The sun's weak rays gave me just enough light that I could make out my jeans on the floor.

"Want me to throw things in the wash while we do breakfast?"

I turn and look at him with a grin. "You're just trying to keep me naked for another couple hours."

"Can't blame a guy for trying. Did it work?"

His impish grin made me giggle, but I had to focus. One of us had to, anyway. I walked back to him, my jeans dangling from my fingers in one hand. I slid one hand up his chest, resting my fingertips along his jaw as I stepped closer and whispered a single word."

"No."

His gobsmacked expression was hilarious. "What?"

"Mox, sweetie, we need to go back to the arena. We don't have the time to play right now. I need to go home and get my things for work."

"Oh." His face fell, disappointment clear. "You're right, I mean, we can't just stay here all day."

"Hey," I say softly, wrapping my arms around him. "It's only until after work, okay?"

"It's not just that, it's also that I'm supposed to go to my sister's house tonight because it's dinner night."

"Oh. Well, we can always hang after or something."

"No, I think I want to bring you with me."

Say what?

"Mox, you don't need to."

"But I want to."

"How about the next one? You can let your sister know I'm coming instead of just surprising her with me."

"I...I kind of already told her about you." "Say that again?"

"I already told her about you. She likes you and the fact that you give me a hard time."

"Elliot…"

"I know, I know." He runs a hand through his hair, his nervous tic. "But I know she'd like you there, only because she told me I have to bring you. Just come with me?"

"Okay, we'll go. But what should I bring, or what do I wear?"

"It's super casual, and I don't think you'd go wrong with that cheesecake you brought me before. Damn, that was good."

"Okay, so I guess I'm meeting the family tonight."

CHAPTER 24

ELLIOT

MY GUT HAD those nerves like before a playoff game. As I walk up the sidewalk with Ronni's small hand tucked into mine, I try to figure out how this is going to go. I've never introduced Sami and Gabby to anyone I've dated before. This is serious, and I want to have all of my girls together. Ronni's eyes are on me as I walk up to the door, and pause with my hand on the knob, I swear I can feel them on my jaw that I just can't unclench.

"Mox, you good?" I look down at her, her expression soft on mine. "If you're nervous, you don't need to do this, okay?"

"Yeah, I'm good, it's just," I pause, "they mean so much to me, and I try to keep them out of the spotlight. They're the most important people in my life, and they don't need the headache that comes from my shenanigans."

"Your shenanigans have gotten a lot better lately, but I get it. It's a lot to take on, especially if it's not their own choice."

I smile. I love that she gets me without my explanation. "Well, then let's get this show on the road. Oh, also, Gabby's kind of sensitive about the hair thing…"

"Mox," she says, placing her hand over my racing heart. "It's okay. We've got this. I promise."

I take a deep breath and turn the knob. It's now or never. With a hand on the small of her back, I usher her into the house. Sami has some kind of pop music playing on the speakers, and I can hear Gabby talking to her mom in the kitchen.

"Sami, Gabby, we're here!" I bellow, then hear Gabby squeal. We come around the corner and I see Gabby sitting on a barstool, watching her mom cook dinner on the other side of the kitchen island with a book on one hand. Her Ohio State Hockey sweatshirt looked massive on her, but I couldn't tell if it was actually Sami's instead.

"Uncle El!" She reaches out toward me, and I head over to her immediately for a small hug. "I missed you after the game, and I had so much to tell you!"

"Were you planning to yell at me about that tripping penalty? Coach beat you to it, if so."

"Nope. I wanted to talk to you about that missed shot in the 3rd period because you're always whiffing it on the blocker side. You're supposed to work with Robicheaux on that in praccy."

"Where would I be without you, Gabs. Hey, I want you to meet my friend Ronni. Ronni, this is my niece Gabby. She likes to think she can out-coach Coach."

"It's so nice to meet you finally," Ronni says as she comes up beside me, holding her hand out to Gabby. In true Gabby fashion, she bypassed the handshake and dove for a hug instead.

"I forgot to warn you, she's a hugger." Watching two of my favorite girls together made my heart clench.

"Hi Ronni! How has he been behaving, do I need to yell at him for you? I will! He knows better than to talk bad with a lady!" She whips her head back toward me.

"Someone has to coach you, because you can't coach your-self for-"

"Gabriella...," Sami's warning tone cut her off. "Quit

talking like you're at the rink. Hi, Ronni, it's so nice to finally meet you!" Sami came around the island, wiping her hands dry on a towel before shaking Ronnie's hand. "I apologize for anything this brat has gotten up to with you. I swear our mother brought us up with manners, even if he acts like he was raised by wolves."

Ronni laughed out loud at their antics, and looked at me with an impish grin. Oh no, she wouldn't...

"Actually, he's been on his best behavior recently, but it wasn't always that way." She leans in toward them and stage whispers, "But did he tell you about the time he sent a frightened intern to bring me coffee because he forgot to do it himself?"

Sami shoots me a look. "Seriously, Elliot, those are not your personal assistants! That's not what you use interns for!"

I hold up my hands in surrender. "In my defense, it was her fault we ran late. Either way, I haven't had to do that since, so I would say I've vastly improved!"

Ronni and Sami share a glance. "Nice try, bro, but it's not flying with us. We know better than to believe that," Sami says with a laugh. "Come on, you can help me set the table, you're just in time. Gabby, would you like to get drinks for Ronni and Elliot?"

"Sure, Mom!" Gabby climbs down from the barstool and heads over toward the refrigerator.

We fall into the comfortable routine of a family dinner, and I'm thrilled with how Ronni just feels so natural sitting here between my niece and sister. Is this what I've been missing out on, should I have figured out this is what I needed in my life sooner? Maybe my career wouldn't be in danger if I had skipped out on the drama that Lacey gave me and fell for a straight laced girl...woah. Have I really fallen for her?

I look up from my glass at Ronni, her head tilted at me like she's waiting on something.

"What's up?" I ask after a small cough.

Sami looks at me with wide eyes. "I asked you what your plans were for the Foundation Ball. You haven't RSVP'ed yet."

"Oh, well, I hadn't gotten that far yet. I suppose I should, they need head counts and names for seating and all that, right?"

"Not only that, but they're still looking for donations for the auction. What are you putting in? I have some ideas if you need them," Ronni chimed in.

"I had a few ideas, and I have a few game day things set aside. Bishop and some of the single guys are auctioning off exclusive events, like a day at the rink or dinner with them. It's an idea, and it might get some big donations.

"Mama, may I be excused? I'm tired," Gabby chimes in. I notice that the big energy she started dinner with has faded, and she's pale.

"Do you need a hand, Coach?" I ask Gabby quietly, and slowly edge out of my seat. She glances down at the table, frowning a bit, before nodding at me. I come around, gather her small frame in my arms and carry her toward her room.

"It's been a busy day, Princess," I murmur toward her as I reach her door. I set her carefully on her mattress, then start to pull the comforter down for her.

She slides over under the covers and I carefully lay them back over top of her.

"Uncle El? I really like Ronni," she whispers, as her eyes droop.

I smile at her. "I really like her too." "Will you keep her?"

"As long as she'll let me, Gabs."

She smiles with her eyes closed, and then her face relaxes into the exhausted sleep I've grown accustomed to over the course of her illness.

"Sleep tight, Princess Buttercup."

I slowly ease my way out of her room, quietly sliding the

door into the frame before heading back to the dining room. Ronni and Sami both look up at me as I walk in, stopping their conversation before I can hear it.

"She's all tucked in, I don't know if her head even hit the pillow before she was out. This latest round is really knocking her for a loop."

Sami looks at me somberly. "It is, and it kills me to see it, but the doctors said earlier this week that her numbers were looking promising."

"That's amazing news, Sami," I say. "Any luck on the donor search?" Ronni's eyes ping pong between the two of us.

I can see the gears turning in her head, as she tries to figure out what we're talking about. I have a moment here I contemplate if now is the time to info dump on her, but Sami takes the decision away from me.

"I take it he didn't tell you beforehand? Dumb jock," Sami chuckles humorlessly. "Gabby has leukemia, and has been in treatment for the last year. He's her favorite transport and treatment buddy, but he doesn't tell anyone he's taking her. Let me guess, he gave you a blocked off schedule with zero explanation?"

"Yeah, actually, he did," Ronni says, looking at me with a head tilt. "Why haven't you said anything, you could have told me. God, I was so pissed at you for those date blocks!"

I run a shaky hand through my hair, and cringe.

Sami butts in before I can answer. "Oh, he says he has reasons. He doesn't want it to become a publicity stunt, or to draw unwanted attention to Gabby, which I get. But it's okay to tell people." Sami looks my way again. "Seriously, dude, your communication skills suck."

"Come on, they're not all bad."

"Yeah, they kind of are," Ronni chimes in, breaking up our argument. I look on in shock as they start breaking down my character failures.

"Awesome. My girlfriend and sister are ganging up on me. Who ordered this? I sure didn't!"

"Aw, El, it's not that bad," Sami admonishes. "Be grateful we like each other!"

"She does have a point, it's much nicer when everyone likes each other."

"Snow Queen, you didn't even like me until like three weeks ago, so I don't know if your statement holds firm."

"I liked you as a coworker, I just didn't like the crap you put me through to find you, clean up your reputation, or try to put a spin on your ex-girlfriends' statements." I side-eye her a little. "Okay, I also didn't like how your name was also attached to every tabloid story from the team, it made my job too hard." My head turns to her fully now. "Okay, and I also didn't like how you specifically avoided all of my events and news stories. Is that better?"

"And now the truth comes out." Sami's statement breaks our staring contest. "So all you had to do was behave yourself and you wouldn't have been in hot water? Silly boy, you do this shit to yourself!" Her chuckle is infectious, even if she is giving me a hard time.

"If I wanted to be chirped at after dinner, I'd go to Robey's house. I may not understand half of them, but at least they'd be expected."

"It's all in love, bro. We just want what's best for you."

"Yeah, yeah, I know," I laugh.

The girls continued chatting as I sat back, taking

it all in. Maybe, after all the dust settles, I can see about making this a regular occurrence. Ronni fit in seamlessly with my family, it's like she belonged here the entire time.

I could see us doing this more often together.

CHAPTER 25

VERONICA

PERHAPS I MISJUDGED Elliot "my freaking secret boyfriend" Moxley. I can't say it too loudly and I definitely couldn't make it obvious at work, but how did I not know that he had all the makings of "best boyfriend" ever? Sure, he had a sketchy press history. Yes, he even spaced and almost missed out on another one of my events last week; he had a good excuse, he saw a peewee player at the skate shop and got sidetracked helping her lace in a fresh pair of skates and pick out new gear. But as irritated as I was, he made it up to me by staying a solid hour later than originally planned! The fact that he took me out later for a candlelit dinner in a private dining room didn't play into that at all. He had a good heart, and it showed.

All of this led to us where we are now, camping out on his couch, my head pillowed on his shoulder and my legs thrown over his while watching some campy horror flick together. His fingers dance through my curls as I lean in closer to him with the building suspense on the screen. As the villain pops out of the darkness and the heroine screams, I cringe and curl in closer.

"You good?" He whispered against my temple.

Solid and unflustered, he pulls me closer to him. "Yeah, that's actually my favorite part. The jump scare. It's how you know it's a good movie." I lean forward, grabbing the bowl of popcorn from the coffee table before settling back into the crook of his arm. He drops his free hand into the bowl while his arm around me held me a little tighter.

"Well, I'll just have to protect you from the monsters then." There's this moment where the on-screen action blurs away into nothing, we are just existing in this bubble alone. As he leans down to kiss me, a loud scream erupts from the screen and we both jump, jostling the bowl and raining popcorn across our legs.

"Wow, my hero," I giggle, as he cringes and scoops the loose pieces into his hands. "I can dig out your vacuum."

"Nah, don't worry about it. I honestly don't know where it is. I have someone come in on the regular and clean."

"So you're really never here, are you?"

"Nah, this is the most time I've ever spent in my place. I'm usually hanging with Sami and Gabby, or on the road, or at the rink. I really only had it to keep my stuff separate from theirs and have a potential place to hang with the guys or, um… well, you know." He cringed. "Sorry. Also, on the off chance I ever end up traded, it would make moving easier. Granted, it did make coming home after hanging with the guys easier, no explanations needed."

"That's fair. I mean, I know you haven't been a saint. I fielded the questions at the press conferences for you, after all."

"I know, it's just that I regret some of my past choices. You wouldn't have had to deal with the press conferences if I was a responsible adult, and I do feel bad about that. No wonder you hated me," he laughs, scooping the last of the popcorn back up.

"I didn't hate you," I confess. "Frustration was probably as far as I got, if I'm totally honest. I mean, I had to work harder to fix you than anyone else. The rest of the guys attempted to keep their shenanigans to a limit, or at least to a group activity."

"Like the goalies?"

"Exactly, like the goalies. That took a lot for us to maneuver through, but it was a one-shot ordeal for them all, and they've been on their best behavior since then."

"That's just because Bishop threatened them with severe bodily harm if they stepped out of line. He didn't appreciate how it went down. They didn't want to see what he would come up with as a punishment."

"Oh, I could only imagine what he came up with. Rumor has it he visits a certain members-only club downtown." Elliot's face froze. "Wait, is that not a rumor?"

"You don't know anything about that, Ronni. Keep quiet about that one. Okay?"

"Absolutely, I wouldn't say anything about that, anyway. But seriously? The interns are talking about it."

"Please do what you can to distract them from that. He'll shit if he finds out about it."

"Will do. His secret is safe with me."

The movie played on, my head growing heavy. The comfort I got from just being near Elliot lulling me into a calm.

"You falling asleep on me, Snow Queen?" He dropped a soft kiss against my forehead, and I realize the credits were running on the screen.

"I guess so." I stretch a bit and before I could get up, Elliot hoisted me up into his arms and started carrying me across the living room.

"What are you doing? I can walk, you know," I started to wiggle, only for him to tighten his hold on me.

"I'm taking you to bed, duh."

"I should really head back home," I start to protest, but he gives me a look. "We both have work tomorrow, you have a game tomorrow night."

"And you're going to crash her tonight. You have time to go home tomorrow morning before going in. Just humor me, I'd feel better if you stayed. You're dead on your feet. Plus, I'm not ready to say goodbye."

My heart melts, the statement so unbelievably sweet. I surrender to his demands, allowing him to set me on the edge of his bed while he digs out a shirt and boxers for me to sleep in. We both prepare for bed and slide beneath the covers, snuggled close together.

"This is the perfect way to end the day," I murmur sleepily against him as he pulls me close.

"Agreed, that's why I insisted you stay." A warm hand slid up and down my spine as he dropped a kiss to the top of my head. "I get my best sleep with you around. You're like my good luck charm."

"That's probably the dumbest thing I've heard, but I'll take it." I sigh contentedly as that hand slid up, and down, slowly dipping fingers at the waistband, before sliding back up again. "That's going to put me to sleep," I mumble as he proceeded to make the same motion again.

"That's just fine. Sleep tight, Snow Queen."

I try to say something back before I drop into sleep, his light touch relaxing me as I drift off.

CHAPTER 26

ELLIOT

LIFE IS SO FUCKING GOOD. I have an amazing girlfriend, my stats look great, we aren't terribly far out of playoff contention, and Gabby is on a good upswing with her health. Nothing can bring me down, and I mean nothing.

I'm jamming to a song in my head that played the other night while Ronni stayed over with me and I'm pretty sure it's my new favorite song ever. Riding the elevator upstairs, all I could think of was that Ronni is coming over again tonight and she said she'd actually bring over things to leave. Leaving her things in my bathroom felt an awful lot like getting tapped as MVP, so I'm not mad about it!

The doorman had flagged me down to let me know that a young woman had gone upstairs to see me before I entered the elevator, and I almost couldn't contain my excitement to see Ronni's face when I got off the elevator. The elevator doors open on my floor and I walk down the hall until I see someone else in the hall that definitely isn't Ronni. That's unusual, I thought, because most of the time my floor is empty at this time of the day. My gut drops, I realize I know who it is and I really, really do not want to deal with this now.

"Hey, Mox," Lacey says as I approach my door. "Long time no see, huh?"

"Yeah, about that. You shouldn't be here. How did you even get in here?"

"Doorman didn't stop me," she shrugs it off like her appearance here isn't that big of a deal.

"Pity. I'll need to fix that." I shove my hands in my pockets and lean against the wall across from my door. "I'm serious, Lacey, I don't want you here, and you need to leave."

"I just wanted to talk to you. I'm sorry about a couple months ago, I was mad and I said things I didn't mean."

Funny, I thought, *you didn't regret signing that check.*

"You nearly got me traded because I said I needed to focus on my career. I'm still trying to fix that problem with my career, by the way."

"Oh yeah, I saw that. Great job on picking yourself up, everyone loves a good redemption arc."

"I wouldn't have needed a 'redemption arc' if you would have kept our private things private! Jesus, Lacey, do you have any idea what you've done?"

"I know I've been bad. But I'm sorry it hurt your career. I just wanted to teach you a lesson."

"And what, exactly, did you think I needed to learn about this? Don't trust anyone with anything private? Congratulations, it worked."

"No." She stared at me as if my inability to figure this out was an insult. "You needed to learn that letting go of me was the worst thing you could have done. The fact that your other exes chimed in with me was unexpected."

"This makes no sense. Why? Why would you think that I'd ever be okay with this, or forgive you?"

I should be ashamed of this argument in the hallway, but I don't dare let her in my apartment.

Something just tells me that it wouldn't go well. I can feel my heart racing, the anger and anxiety making my thoughts blur. There's cameras here, right? So I'll be okay.

Again, she gives me that smile I used to get in public with her. All teeth and glowing adoration, but it doesn't reach her eyes. "Because, Elliot, I didn't release everything."

"Don't you dare."

"Or what, Elliot? What will you do? Will you send your little PR princess after me to clean up your mess again?"

"Ronni has better things to do than try to clean up after you. She's busted her ass fixing the damage you've done."

"Oh, you're on a first name basis with her now? That's an interesting turn of events."

Fuck. She's like a shark scenting blood in the water.

"Yeah, and? If it wasn't for your off-season bullshit, she would have had better things to do than babysit me to put my reputation back in order."

"I'm sure that's not all she was doing with you."

"You don't know what you're talking about, Lacey. Stop trying to cause more trouble."

"Oh, really? So you aren't banging your PR girl, Elliot? Care to take a bet on that?"

"No, I don't, because-"

"Because you're banging your PR girl. Just say it. You turned into one of those guys. You wouldn't let me be your PR girl because it would be, what did you call it, a power imbalance? A conflict of interest? But it's different with her because she's already in PR? I'm sure HR would love to hear about this one."

"Stop it, Lacey. You've done enough damage. Destroy whatever you think you have on me, and let it go. We're done. If we weren't before, we definitely are now. There's no way I'm letting you anywhere near my life after the last six months."

"You're making a massive mistake here, Elliot. You're going to find out."

I watch her storm down the hallway and wait for her to get into the elevator before I head into my apartment, throwing the deadbolt and security chain across the door for good measure.

CHAPTER 27

VERONICA

SOMETHING FELT OFF TODAY. Normally, I wouldn't be able to get this man to shut up, and instead I have gotten nothing from him but short answers. The answers weren't cold, but just lacking.

"Are you okay?" I ask him for what felt like the tenth time since we came back from the arena. We are curled up in his bed, my head tucked against his shoulder.

"Yeah," he responds, his fingers running through my curls. "I'm just tired and not in a great headspace. But having you here helps."

"That's so sweet," I murmur, leaning up to kiss him softly. "You know you can talk to me about anything, right? If it helps to put you in a better mindset."

"I know, and I appreciate it." He pulls me closer, my top leg laying across his, as he lifts me across to straddle him. "It's nothing you need to worry about, I'm just in a funk. But maybe you can get me out of it?"

"Avoidance doesn't fix it, you know." I slide my hands up his chest as I lean forward, pressing my lips to his. He pulls his arms around me, holding me down against him as he deepened the kiss on me.

"No, but it feels a hell of a lot better than overthinking it. I'll be okay, I just need to work through this. It's nothing you need to worry about, I can fix it myself."

"Are you sure?" I sit up, breaking contact between us momentarily. "I don't want you to deal with it alone if you don't need to. I'm happy to help you out."

"I know. I'll handle this one myself. Besides, I have something better to do with you at the moment."

I squeal as he banded an arm around my middle, twisted, and presses me down into the mattress in a second. Without missing a beat, his lips are on me again.

Seriously, I have to give the man credit. He's single-minded in distraction. No wonder he has impeccable shot percentages.

CHAPTER 28

ELLIOT

I KNOW I should have told Ronni that Lacey knows about us, even though I still don't know how. I don't want to get her upset if I don't need to, and honestly, what can she really have on us? That's just surreal. We haven't gone into a public setting that wasn't club sanctioned, and we show up at my place or hers separately. So seriously, I doubt Lacey has anything and is just trying to weasel her way back in. It's not happening. I know what I had then and I know what I have now, and the tradeoff isn't worth it. I'm happy now. Despite that, my gut has a weird knot in it as I wonder if telling Ronni would be helpful in the end.

My silverware dances back and forth on my fingertips as I fiddle with them. It's nervous energy, but I'm trying to still smile and give that cool and relaxed vibe that she deserves. After all the stress and work over the last few months, I think we've finally fixed my reputation issues upstairs, and I couldn't be happier.

The execs came down to the locker room after practice the other day and commented on how nice it was to see positive news stories from me instead of last season's drama. I agree, it's easier to just breathe and be myself now. No extra photo shoots at the last minute, Ronni gives ample scheduling for me. She really has my best interests at heart and I told them so. She needs a raise, a promotion, something. She's working some serious magic for me.

"You okay over there, El?" I look up to see Ronni looking at me, her brows down-turned in concern. "We don't have to do this tonight if you're tired. You have some big games coming up."

"No, I'm good, I'm just up in my head again. Come here." I motion to her, pulling her closer to me on the couch. "I just need to spend some time with my girl, I think that will fix it."

"Sweet talker," she chides, while snuggling in tighter to me. We have a cheesy movie on the television but I can't even focus on it. It's just background noise, kind of like every time we get together. The entire world could burn down around us and I'm pretty sure we would both be blind to it. All I can do is focus on her, and it feels like the same is at play for her, too.

"Is it working?"

"Hmm, for now. But I'm serious, El, you can talk to me if it will help."

She'd given me an in to discuss, and I know I should take it, but the words are jammed in my throat.

Fucking say something, quit being a chickenshit, a rookie has more balls than this.

Instead, I just lean over and place a kiss on her forehead. I'll tell her later. I don't want to mess this up, and I don't think she'll like this at all.

It makes my heart race to consider how it could play out if I told her that just the other day, Lacey stood on my doorstep. The same doorstep she was just on a couple hours ago. I visualize how her face would fall, the disappointment on her face, it would be like the off-season all over again and I couldn't dare see that look on her face. No matter what. No, I'll keep it to myself. Things are better than before, and honestly, what damage could Lacey really do at this point? I'd cleared my conscience, and cleaned up my act.

I have come too far to go back into that swamp with Lacey again. No. She didn't matter anymore. She wouldn't hurt us. We are moving forward, away from the gossip mags and tell-all's. That was all in my past, and my past would not define me or break me down.

Ronni was my future, and we have nowhere to go from here but up. I can't stop the nervous energy in my gut like something was about to happen.

CHAPTER 29

VERONICA

I WAKE up in an empty bed, Elliot's side still a little warm. I smile, reminiscing about the night before. When he isn't irritating the shit out of me at work, he's actually a really great guy. I stretch, burrowing underneath the covers that still smell like him and relishing in the achy muscles as I moved.

The alarm interrupts me, and I groan, knowing I have to eventually go to my place. I pick up my phone from his nightstand, where he had apparently plugged it in before he left. My screen lights up with a recent incoming text notification underneath the cheerful "6:00" over top of my wallpaper.

I grin as I see Elliot's name. The text is simple:

Moxley: Hey, Snow Queen. I didn't have the heart to wake you up before I left for the rink. Make yourself at home. I have fresh creamer in the fridge too. I miss you already, you know that?

My heart leaped in my chest. It isn't fair for him to be so thoughtful. With a sigh, I climb out of bed, heading into the bathroom to shower. His interior designer didn't get paid enough for this monstrosity. The warm water works wonders on my cobwebbed brain and aching muscles, and I hope that his shampoo and conditioner won't totally wreck my hair.

Climbing out of the shower made me sad, but had to be done. His towels felt like fluffy clouds, and I slowly got ready. Heading into the bedroom to steal one of his sweatshirts, I freeze. I'm not alone.

I look at the bed, the one that I was in alone until half an hour ago, and see *her* there.

"Lacey. What are you doing here?" I keep my tone light and conversational, neutral.

"Oh hi, you must be the new girl. Looks like he moved quickly," she notes, never looking up from her phone. "I noticed he busted out the toy box. So nice of him to share." She looks up at me finally. "Although kind of surprised he dropped that all on you. I mean, you don't strike me as the type to color outside of the lines."

"Elliot will be back any minute now," I warn, hoping that I say it with enough confidence for her to believe me.

"No he won't. He left for morning skate at 5 sharp, and he won't come in the door for another hour at least." Her saccharine smile doesn't fade, her eyes never dropping from me. "So, spicy friendship bracelets, huh? That's cool. Did he tell you he likes to…"

I feel and hear my pulse roaring in my skull as she keeps talking. I'm having a nightmare, it's just a dream, I tell myself repeatedly as she kept talking.

She points out the toy box under his nightstand and describes what was in it. She gave explicitly detailed scenes they played, including constructive notes on what did and did not work. And the whole time I was frozen, staring at her as she kept going, and going.

"Stop it!" I scream. Without thinking, I run for the door, barefoot. I don't even care about the temperature outside. I just run as fast as I could, skipping the elevator and launching myself down the emergency stairs, bursting out of the stair-well door without looking.

The lobby across from me was mostly empty, so I push myself into a sprint. My vision narrows around me as I entered the spacious entryway before running bodily into Elliot at the door.

"Ronni? What are you doing down here?" His questions are soft, his hands gentle as he grasped my shoulders, keeping me upright as I spin away from him.

"No. I'm not…I can't stay here." I shove uselessly against his chest as he keeps me upright and also from running.

"What's wrong? I don't understand. Please, just look at me," he begs. "Talk to me, why are you running?"

"Ask your girlfriend." I spat the words at him, struggling against his hold. I'm only vaguely aware of conversations around us, people watching as we stand and struggle in each others' hold.

"I *am* asking my girlfriend. She's trying to run away from me."

"Just go upstairs, Elliot. I should have known better." His shock loosened his grip enough that I could step away from him and continue toward the door. I don't look back as I walked out onto the cold sidewalk, flag down a cab, and go back home alone.

Watching his building shrink behind me, I feel my heart shatter. I knew better than to get attached to someone in sports, and I did it anyway. I learned my lesson the hard way.

CHAPTER 30

ELLIOT

IT HAS BEEN three weeks since I last saw Ronni alone. She won't talk to me. Any messages between us are relayed through Jess or, oddly enough, from Bishop. I'm still not sure how he came into play with this twisted game of telephone, but they were at least trying to communicate for me. I still don't know what was said, or why Ronni ran out the way she did. I knew I should have changed my locks after I broke up with Lacey, but just assumed that the months of silence meant I was good. Why, why did she have to show up now?

I have been attending all the events solo or with one of the PR interns, but I never lay eyes on the woman I love. I have a gut feeling Lacey has something to do with this. I didn't believe her when she said nothing happened, I never have. I kicked her out and had building security block her, of course after I retrieved my key. Just to be safe I called maintenance to change all the locks immediately.

I'm dumb. I'm still kicking myself. Sami laid into me hard about it, because for once, she could tell I had someone in my corner for the right reasons. Gabby hasn't forgiven me for taking away her newest reading buddy.

Honestly, I feel the same, Gabs.

I'm going through the motions on ice, and my game sucks. Coach called me out on it after practice today and everything he said is the same shit I've said to myself out there.

Get your shit together, Moxley, before they move you to another city.

This isn't my first breakup, so why is it hitting me so damn hard this time? I know why, if I'm being totally honest with myself. I care more this time than I ever have in the past. Ronni is my everything. I want her in my life in ways that I couldn't wrap my head around.

I love her. I know it in my soul, feel it in my bones. There has to be a way to fix this because I can't see my life without her in it.

CHAPTER 31

WALKING into work today didn't hurt nearly as bad as the last dozen mornings, but I still wish they would cover up Elliot "I'm a goddamn idiot" Moxley's freakishly gorgeous mug with something or someone else. I now know the route that takes me around the arena and to my office with minimal visuals of his photos. It was a stupid idea to ever get attached to someone who is the face of the entire franchise. It's freaking everywhere, there is no escape.

At my desk, I'm mindlessly rolling my favorite pen across my desk calendar, from one side of my keyboard to the next, while staring blankly at my screen. I'm supposed to be doing player blurbs for the social media posts in the coming weeks to help Jess out. If I'm being totally honest with myself I'm avoiding anything to do with Elliot–no, Moxley–because just seeing him smile in a video makes my chest ache.

Jess is in her cubicle talking to someone who is apparently in the room. They're trying to be quiet, I can tell, but I can still make out her voice and the deeper timbre of someone. I peek around the edge of my cubicle and look toward hers, seeing a large man's back within the opening of her space.

"She's not going to go for this, you know," Jess whispers at the mystery man.

"We need to do something, they're both miserable and I'm tired of him moping around the locker room."

Not a mystery man; it's Val Bishop. I should've known.

"She's never been like this before, but I don't know…"

"You two know I can hear you, right?" I grumble.

Their conversation screeches to a halt. It isn't fair. What did I do wrong? Why do I get the dumb jock who doesn't care about what's going on up here?

"It's all in love, really," Jessica tries to persuade me.

"Love is dumb. Don't go there." My eyebrow raised at Bishop's argument. "Seriously though, neither of you are coping well. Do what we do on the ice. Drop the gloves, get it worked out of your system, spend a couple minutes in the sin bin, and move on to the next faceoff."

"I don't think that's going to solve this one, Bishop."

"Giving each other the silent treatment isn't solving anything either. I may be a dumb hockey player, but at least I know how to use my words like a grownup. Go talk to him. Damnit, you two are so bullheaded."

"There's nothing to talk about, Bishop. He made a series of mistakes that led to his ex practically holding me hostage in his apartment while forcing me to listen to stories of their history and the fact that she had been let into his apartment a mere handful of days before that and he didn't even have the common decency to warn me or even let me know. He didn't trust me knowing that his ex could show up at his place. Telling me anything personal was completely unheard of for him. Please, tell me why I should be A-OK with all of this?" I hear the shrillness of my voice the more I talked but I couldn't be bothered to control myself.

"I didn't say it was okay, Ronni," he says, in a soft tone. He approaches me slowly, like one would to a stray animal. "I said you two need to talk and get this out of your system before one of you explodes. Talk to the man, yell at him if you need to. It will help."

"It won't help. The only thing that will help is getting his face off the glass and getting to the end of the season. I can't deal with this anymore." I move to get up from my desk. "I'm going to set up the press office over the ice for tonight's game. I'll catch you later, Jess. Have a good game tonight, Bishop."

Before either one can protest, I head out the door. Maybe the silence of the empty arena will give me the peace that I need.

CHAPTER 32

A PLAYER KNOWS when things feel wrong, and today, it all feels wrong. I walked into the arena like I always do, I put my socks and skates on in the same order, I even ate the same pre-game snack I've eaten every game since I played in mites. Nothing made the churning in my gut better though. I know why I feel off, but there's nothing I can do about it. Ronni isn't here, or if she is, she's not doing her usual work with Jess.

Breathing exercises in the tunnel didn't change my outlook, so I focused on the warmup. Something has to get me out of this funk, because this game is too damn important. If we win, we have a guaranteed spot in the playoffs; if we lose, we hope the team up north drops a game to keep us out of jeopardy. My warm up laps feel solid, my skates are smooth, and I drop into stretches beside Bishop. We're looking over at the other team, watching their warm up shots on their goalie and watching for weaknesses.

"Boone hesitates before he shoots," Bishop nods toward their goal where a forward is taking a warm-up shot. "Watch that for a turnover chance." He shifts his stretch to point toward a defenseman. "Linkov is favoring that left knee again when he skates." I nod back as I deepen a stretch. "Rockwell's weak on the blocker side. It's not your preferred angle, but you might have goal opportunities there." I grunt in response and let my eyes wander to our bench. Jess and some new intern are standing with Coach, but still Ronni is nowhere to be seen. "Moxley. Pay fucking attention."

"Trying," I grumble.

"No, you're not. You're looking for Ronni. Knock it off and focus. You can look for her after the game. I need you on your A-game. Get it fucking together."

I growl and watched the Generals warm up. I'm so annoyed at Kane Blackwood staring me down across the ice. We used to be best friends in high school, lived together in college, but he cut me off after our farewell graduation party. I've only seen him on opposing teams ever since. He never says a word to me, and I don't know why.

The buzzer sounded for the end of warmups, signaling that it was time to go back to our respective benches and then prepare for the national anthem. The crowd was amped up, and while that usually got me wound up pre-game, today I just couldn't feel it.

With the anthem and team introductions completed, all I can do is line up for faceoff at center ice. I take my position, looking on as Kane lines up across from me, his dark eyes narrowed. He looks like he did when he was itching to scrap, and it was a look I had enjoyed watching from the side; seeing it in front of me was not as fun, though.

"Blackwood," I greet, as cordially as one can at faceoff.

"Fuck off, Moxley," he growls in return. The shock of his insult put me at a disadvantage as the puck drops, and he gathers it with his stick before I could react.

Cursing, I skate into my zone, chasing his winger who was juggling the puck on his stick. Bishop crouched, watching the shift of the puck from in front of the net. He would chew me out for this later. I check the winger, knocking him off-kilter and swiping the puck away, smacking it toward Robicheaux before shifting on my skates and skating back into our offensive end. I see Kane in my peripheral, skating hard on my stick side as Roby passed me the puck, seeing that I was on the goalie's weak side.

I take my shot, keeping my eyes trained on the puck as it went airborne on a trajectory to go just above the goalie's stick. He blocks, the puck bouncing off of his blocker and bouncing awkwardly back toward the boards. I chase it down, keeping Kane beside me as we both headed the same way. We collide at the boards, both of us digging for the puck to take control. He throws an elbow as he shifts his weight to shove me away, and I shove back at him in retaliation.

"Jesus, Kane, it's not that damn serious," I wheeze a bit as my lungs inflated.

"The hell it's not, back off, Mox." He shoves me again as I swipe the puck away from us and I watch it go under control of my lineman.

He races away from me, his stick hooking the back of my calf but going unseen by the referee. I cringe and followed, trying to skate off the cramp building in the muscle from the impact. On and on our lines battled throughout the period, neither team giving anything away as the period crawled to an end.

I crumple onto the bench in the locker room after the first period of play. One down, two to go, I think as I take a swig of sports drink. I just want this game to end already. Bishop, who was the last in the locker room, drops beside me.

"Playing in the peewee's again?" His chirp stings, if I'm honest.

"Not for lack of trying," I grumble. "I swear playing Kane Blackwood is like taking down a hornet's nest. Not fun, feels kind of dangerous, and you know you're going to get stung before the day is out."

"I still don't know what you did to him in the minors, but he plays like he has a chip on his shoulder."

"Beats me. We played great together until we didn't."

"Just play clean. I know he tries to egg you into fights but just play a clean game."

"Yeah, I know."

I relax a bit and try to get my muscles to relax. This game is going to kill me at this rate. I just want it to be over with. A door opens on the other side of the locker room and I look up with just enough time to watch Ronni walk out of Coach's office, and out the door without even a second glance back at me. Coach walks out just behind her, looks at my face, and scowls.

"Moxley! Get your ass in my office. Now!"

Without another word, I waddle that direction on my skates, leaving Bishop and the team staring after me.

"Hey, Coach," I call as I cross the threshold, opting to stand over the chair and not try to sit in my gear.

"Can you stop staring down the PR team Jesus Christ, it's like High School Musical around here. Too much freaking emotion! Get your head back into the goddamn game, you got it?"

"Got it, sorry, Coach." I turn toward the door. "Is that all?"

"No. I wanted to let you know I saw the way you and Blackwood were going at it on the ice, just watch yourself, okay? One wrong move and you might be suspended. They've been playing aggressive this season and the refs have had enough. I don't want you to get caught holding the bag for the penalties."

"Cool deal. Thanks."

"Oh, and Mox?" He paused until I looked at him. "She'll come around, just give her some time. I know it sucks but just keep doing what you're doing."

I nod and walk out, stewing in my tormented feelings.

Second period leaves me ragged and on the verge of throwing my gear. For every shot I line up, Kane was right there. We may not have played together on the same team in recent years, but that teammate ESP was still working. I grit my teeth as we took the ice for the third period, and I just begged whichever deity oversaw our team that it would be quick, easy, and maybe a little painless. Apparently we weren't being watched tonight.

Four minutes into the period, Robey is taken down by a dirty hit, and went back to the trainers. I see red. Kane Blackwood is going down for this, regardless. I skate square into his face, lose all of my cool, and then promptly drop gloves and throw the first punch. I don't care about my career, the suspension, whatever "optics" Ronni would be pissed about. It feels so good to smash his face a little bit. He needed it.

As I march to the locker room, I can hear her voice in my ear. I can hear her lecturing me on how I had one job, and all I had to do was behave.

Knowing what that sounded like, I didn't care. At least I could hear her voice, even if I made it all up in my head.

"VERONICA SNOW. I know. I'll get right on it. Will do, thanks." I hung up the phone for the hundredth time today. My voice felt scratchy from talking so much, and repeating the same phrases over and over again.

No Comment. That is a private matter. Mr. Moxley will address the press at a later date. I'll fix it. I'm taking care of that.

Every time I picked up my phone today, it was the same thing. Calls from outside the arena asking about Elliot, what he was going to do, if the team was keeping him. Calls coming from inside the arena, asking what the hell was going on and what could I do to fix it.

I know what I could do to fix it. I know what my heart wanted me to do to make this whole nightmare stop and I can't do a damn thing about it. What it want is for me to go running into Elliot's arms, asking him what went wrong, and maybe—just maybe—we could talk our way through this.

My brain is on a different course though.

Logically I knew I made the right decision to walk out of the apartment that day. Sitting around his apartment hearing his ex talk about all the things he had said or done during their relationship was not on my list of ideal things to do. So I left. I know he wanted to talk to me, I mean, I had a phone full of unanswered calls and text messages begging me for a moment to explain. I said what I needed to say, that perhaps during the season wasn't the best time to bend all of my rules and date a professional hockey player. Perhaps dating a professional hockey player with an ex like Lacey was a really, terrible idea.

I needed to focus on work and attempting to fix the dumpster fire that was Elliot Moxley's professional career, all while not communicating with him at all. I couldn't deal with it. Distance, that's what I needed. Jess had my back, even if she didn't understand or agree with me. She took up the communication side for me, running as middle-man between us after last night.

Despite that, it hurt.

"Ronni," Michael's voice calls out to me from his office doorway, and I groan before dropping my head backwards.

"On my way, Michael." I stand up, smoothing out the wrinkles on my skirt, gather my planner, and head toward him. I don't know what he needed to say, but I figure if my phone was blowing up like this, then he had to be hearing it as well. Or worse.

Walking into Michael's office, I shouldn't have been surprised to see the commissioner standing near the window, or his personal assistant sitting in the chair in the corner of Michael's office with a notepad at the ready. I shoot her a tight smile and sit at the chair across from her.

Michael closes the office door before sitting in a chair beside me, and the three of us stay silent as the commissioner comes over.

"Ronni, I know that this looks like an ambush, but I promise that we're just here to support. We have some questions and we're hoping we can fix some of the press before we have to reassess the situation."

"If this is regarding Mr. Moxley's antics on ice, I could not have predicted that kind of behavior, and that wasn't part of the discussions we had about his image improvement," I start. They really couldn't think that the fight was my problem…could they?

"We understand that," the commissioner starts. "We really don't think you could have done anything regarding that. Our concern though, is that maybe this is getting too big for you to handle."

"I'm fine. It's fine." I shoot a look at Michael. "Is there any reason that you two believe that I'm not handling the situation?"

Michael looked down at the ground, his tell that he was about to deliver bad news. "I know you've had Jess relaying for you the last week or so."

"So you also know that the 'last week or so' I've been heavier on the foundation planning than she has, and logistically it worked out better for us to handle those portions as we did. Has Mr. Moxley said that she did not take care of the situation as I would have?"

"It's not that, Ronni. It's just a matter of," he looked toward the commissioner for backup. "Has he been inappropriate with you? Is that why you two are not talking? You know you can tell us if he's being unprofessional."

"What's 'unprofessional,' Michael, is assuming I can't handle the task handed to me. It's handled. From here on out he will be my sole focus. Is that what you need to hear?"

"That's not what we're saying at all," the commissioner chimes in. "But it does seem like this may be a bit much for one person to take on, and with his suspension as it is, we had concerns that maybe the on-ice hostility was also off-ice."

I stare the commissioner square in the eye. "Elliot Moxley has been a perfect gentleman for me and a consummate team player. Last night was the first time in a long time that I saw any kind of hostility or untoward behavior toward anyone. It is my hope that in the next three weeks, while he is benched, that I can continue to repair his reputation as requested. Even with this slight setback, I refuse to give up on him. Is that sufficient?"

"That's fine, Ronni. Thanks for clarifying."

"You're welcome. Now, if there's nothing else, I have been busy fielding phone calls from the press all morning about the suspension announcement. I would like to get those cleaned up before I check back in with our team captain and get him back on the road to redemption." With that said, I stand, ignoring my shaky knees, and walk out the door.

"ELLIOT MOXLEY IS in hot water and his contract renewal could be in jeopardy, rumors say. The 27-year-old center is currently sitting out a five game suspension for this late hit on a Las Vegas Generals player…"

I growl and change the channel, going to the next sports channel in the sequence.

"…requesting anonymity, a source from within the Ice Wolves states that there is a lack of confidence in his ability to keep his personal drama off the ice. It sounds like the Ice Wolves may shop for a new center, and a new captain, when the trade windows open up."

I curse and stab another button on the remote.

"Honestly, JP, if my center behaved like that during one of the most important games of the season, I would reconsider if he was worth it."

The sound cuts out as I shut off the television and just sit in silence, the remote teetering on my denim clad thigh. I look over at Gabby's hospital bed where she's sleeping peacefully at the moment.

I'm glad one of us can.

I flex my bruised hand and cringe as the cuts around my

knuckles ache. I let my temper get the better of me–again–and I had no one to blame but myself. I could have let his words slide off me, just focused on the gameplay, but I couldn't. He pulled Sami into it. I haven't gotten along with him since our early hockey days, and the years apart haven't helped a bit. And why did he know my sister's name, anyway? Asshole, he can keep her name out of his mouth.

I breathe deeply and let it out slowly. I have to let this go, I can't hold on to this frustration and expect to be here when Sami and Gabby need me. My phone dings quietly from beside me and I glance at the screen, expecting to see Bishop's ugly mug on it. I jolt when I realized it's Ronni–no; she has to be Ms. Snow now–and picked up my phone. My throat squeezes shut and I can't even get the words out to give a proper greeting.

"Moxley. I know you're there, I can hear you."

"Hey," I finally whisper. It's gritty sounding, but it's the first word I've been able to say to her in ages.

I hear her sigh. "Look, I know you're at the hospital with Gabby and you're still on suspension, but we need to talk. Can I come see you?"

"Anytime, you don't have to ask. I'll head to my place."

"No, I have to ask. And how about someplace public? I don't want to intrude if Lacey is over at your place."

I growl at that woman's name. "She's not there. I changed the locks and have a restraining order open on her. You're the only one-"

"We're not talking about that, Moxley, this is strictly a business matter. It should have stayed strictly business the whole time."

My eyes drift shut and my head bows in defeat. I knew I should have talked to her sooner, but it just didn't seem right.

"I'm going to be here the rest of the day. Sami is working out some details to get Gabby's paternal side tested as a possible donor. Can," I pause, "will you come over? Gabs misses you too."

"Please don't make this harder on any of us than it needs to be, Elliot. I'm not putting her through this. Can you see me at the coffee shop downstairs in an hour?"

"Fine," I agree, but I don't like it.

She hangs up on me without a goodbye or anything, and I just stare at my lock screen. I have to fix this and I don't really know how at the moment.

CHAPTER 35

VERONICA

PEOPLE WATCHING USED to calm me, but today it's just making me more agitated. Three different couples have walked in just in the last few minutes, with adoring smiles and caring touches toward each other. Elliot, naturally, hasn't shown up yet, and I'm not totally surprised. There's still a few minutes before he's supposed to meet me but I'm early. Like always. If I'd be honest with myself, I was already down here when I called him to meet me. I almost got in the elevator and went up to Gabby's room. Sami had texted me her room number a couple days ago when I checked in on them. While I may not be on speaking terms with him, there's no reason I have to stay silent from them. They didn't lie to me, keep secrets, or put me in a position where an ex could harass me. He did though.

Why couldn't he be squeaky clean like the rest of the players? Why did he have to have the ex hell-bent on ruining his image? Why couldn't he just follow the code of conduct and rules that have been set up for him? I had no answers to this and the only person who would should come out of the elevator any minute now, and walk toward me. I could see him in my mind, striding toward me with that cocky, self-assured grin that he always had. Completely unbothered by anything that was going on around him.

I look up as the elevator dings, the steel doors open, and I gasp in shock. The man who walked toward me was not that man at all. His feet were dragging along the tiles, his usually impeccable clothing a rumpled mess, there's a good day's worth of stubble on his face and dark patches underneath his bloodshot eyes. His hair, which usually has that "effortlessly mussed" look, instead looked as though he ran his fingers through it too many times for the product to hold in place. He looked broken.

My heart clenches as he approaches the table and climbs slowly onto the stool across from me. He doesn't make eye contact; the Elliot I know would hold your gaze and never look away.

"M-Ms. Snow," he whispers, his voice too roughened for anything louder. I watch him lay his hands on the tabletop, his fingers reaching out toward mine like they had a mind of their own. How many times had we sat just like this over the last couple months and thought nothing at all of those fingers searching for mine? As if realizing what he was doing, he pulled his hands back toward himself, sliding them off of the tabletop and into his lap.

"Moxley. Sorry to interrupt your time with Gabby."

"It's okay. She's asleep right now, anyway." He sighs, running a hand over his stubbly cheek. "I missed you."

"Mox, we can't…"

"I'm just saying I missed you. I miss practice with my boys and even hearing Robey's cheesy jokes, if that puts it in a better light for you. I miss the way things were."

I nod, understanding what he meant. "I know. You'll be back before they'll even know you're gone, though."

He stays quiet, biting on his bottom lip as if it would keep the words in. "I miss us, too. I've never felt lonely at home before. I know I need to fix things but, I just wanted you to know that."

"We need to discuss your events coming up after the suspension. I know you didn't intend to set yourself back, but the ejection and suspension did some damage. I need to put together a statement from you to release to the press, and I wanted to put you in touch with a reporter I know to do a softer interview with you than some sports guys throw together."

He gives me a tired smile. "My Snow Queen, you always have an answer for everything, don't you?"

"That's part of what I get paid for, Moxley. I'm not just a babysitter."

His head drops. "I know. And I appreciate it. Send me the times they're available and I'll open myself up. I have nothing but time at the moment. This last round really did a number on Gabby. I suppose if I'm going to punch Kane Blackwood, I picked a good time for it."

I can't stop the chuckle that escapes me. "No, I guess not. Although it would be better if next time there was no punching involved."

We sat, silence enveloping us for a moment. "You know, Gabby stopped talking to me. She said I needed to sit and think about what I've done. It's crazy that a kid is smarter than me sometimes."

"She's a great kid," I agree. "I'd hate to disrupt her today, but I have this for her." I reached into my bag and pulled out a new graphic novel. "I told her about this one, I think she'd like it."

Taking the book, he flips through some pages, pausing at the images of cheerful characters. At least someone is happy, I think glumly.

"I'll give this to her when she wakes up. I'm sure she could use some new reading material."

"Thanks for taking the time to see me, Moxley. We'll get

the PR spin fixed and hopefully get you back on the ice soon. I should go back to the arena though and let you get back to your family." I move to stand and Elliot, in his usual move, stands at the same time.

"Ronni, I mean it, I'm sorry for everything. I miss us, and I want—"

"I know. Now just isn't a great time." I shoot him a sad smile as I walk away. "Please tell Sami and Gabby I said hi, I'll catch you later."

Before I can second guess my actions, I walk back out of the cafe, leaving him behind me.

CHAPTER 36

ELLIOT

STRATEGY IS MY MIDDLE NAME. I have built an entire career on my ability to screen the ice, plot puck angles and trajectories, and calculate the exact second to shoot to catch a goalie off-balance. If I could use that skill on ice, why in the hell can I not figure out how to successfully get out of this situation with Ronni?

The answer is obvious; I have to build her trust back up. It's shaken, and I know I'm at fault. But how can I convince her I'm not some shady motherfucker with trust issues, and that I didn't know what got so out of control?

I get it. I do. I should have told her early on, that Lacey was still bugging me, especially since Ronni was part of the initial damage control press junket. I remember watching her from the conference room, taking notes as I told everything. There should have been some reverberating embarrassment connected to sitting in a room, my agent and lawyer to my left, coach to my right, and across the table from me sat Michael, Ronni, and Jess, attention fully on me as I explained every single article, photo spread, and interview that Lacey had spread like wildfire after our breakup. Photos that I sent her in private went viral on TMZ. Her discussions of our private moments, all laid bare in print format. I remember hearing about sponsors and benefits pulling back support, or requesting a different player for visits. It smarted, sure, to watch my "good boy" persona ripped apart.

And Ronni sat there professionally, asking questions regarding consent, what could or should be said by the team in response. Watching her in her element as she wrote up statements to be released at the press conference was like watching an artist at work. Her words repaired a lot of the cracks and fissures in the public arena. My reputation, while still bruised, seemed to bounce back. The Make-A-Wish requests were coming back. Her subtle placements of me in the team publicity shoots put me back in the fans' view, and the response was favorable.

She didn't have to work that hard for me. I knew she didn't want to, her eye roll whenever she heard about the big press blowup told me she thought it was dumb. So did I, I couldn't blame her. Even so, she dug in and worked her magic. And Lacey was just the latest in a long line of dumb decisions, so my track record wasn't great. I knew it.

Now, here I am. Ronni isn't talking to me, my sister and niece won't acknowledge me unless I prove I can fix this, Lacey and three of my previous exes are apparently on a trash tv junket together to share what it was like being a part of the "Hockey WAGs" scene and what I did or didn't do right as a boyfriend. My life feels like it's falling apart and I'm just stuck in the middle of this shitstorm called my life.

My doorbell ringing interrupts my thoughts, and my heart lurches. Maybe Ronni had come back to tear me a new asshole and forgive me, in no particular order. I trudge over to the door and without looking out the peephole I throw the door open, to see Val Bishop leaning on my door frame.

"Let's go, you sad sack of shit." With that statement, he shoves off the frame and strolls into my apartment like he had a hundred times before. "Damn, your sense of security around here sucks, man. You didn't even know it was me before you opened the door."

"Uh, well, I kind of assumed it would be someone I knew," I stammered, following behind him as he helped himself to a water bottle from my fridge. "What are you doing here?"

"I'm taking you out," he said, as if it was the dumbest question I could have asked. "You've been locked in this apartment and doing nothing. You need fresh air. And who knows? Maybe I know someone who will be at the Sin Bin tonight."

The Sin Bin. My heart lurches at the phrase, as my head remembers how my last visit there went and ended. Ronni sitting in the VIP with me, taking her home, waking up with her curled against me. Even if it was all before we knew what we wanted, it was what felt like our beginning. My brows furrow as I think about going back without her. Or worse, seeing her there with someone else.

"I don't know, Val, I've been avoiding spots like that."

"Right, you've been a good boy, and I think you need a break. Besides, something needs to cheer you up because you're a damned buzzkill in the locker room. We're fucking over it so I'm fixing you."

"Thanks," I mutter dryly while rolling my eyes in his general direction. "If you're not giving me a choice in the matter, at least let me go get changed. Cool?"

He settles deeper into my couch, already changing channels like he owned the thing. I take it as an affirmative and head to my room. I might as well get this over with, I think as I turn to my closet, snagging a white button down and gray slacks from a hanger. Appropriate for any photos I'd be seen in without looking like I'm trying really hard. Even without Ronni here, I could still hear her voice telling me what to wear, what to do, how to behave.

God, I miss her already.

I smooth out my shaggy hair, and heaving another sigh I start toward the living room again. Val was right where I had left him on my couch, but where before he had relaxed into the cushions, now he had leaned forward, elbows on his knees, and glaring at his screen.

"This is as good as it's getting, can we go so and can come back home?"

He shoots me a look, then snags his phone off of my coffee table and shoves it into his pants pocket. "It's better than it was, anyway. If this is how bad you are over a girl, I'd hate to see how rough it is when you lose something big, like The Cup."

"The Cup will always be there. I think I'd handle it better."

"Let's hope we never know. Come on, I have a car waiting."

I follow him downstairs, and we both climb into the back of the waiting SUV. The city passes by the windows and all I can do is count down the minutes until I could come back home, drown my sorrows alone, and wait for another day to pass.

CHAPTER 37

HE'S HERE.

I haven't decided yet if I want to seriously hurt Jess for dragging me here, knowing that this was a major hangout for the players. She had to have known that the odds were high I would either run into him directly, or someone who could tell him I was here. I still didn't stop her though. It is what it is, I'm here now and I can't go home without her.

I can see him sitting on that same couch and behind the same stupid rope as last time. I'm pretty sure the same mountain of a bouncer is standing there, too. I feel ridiculous in this weird strappy dress that Jess told me I needed to wear, I nearly froze on the ride over. The chills have passed and I'm now half-numb with whatever the pink stuff is in this glass.

He hasn't taken his eyes off of me in the last half hour but he also hasn't moved to come see me. This feels like a standoff of some sort. He's out of his mind if he thinks I'm going to be the first to cave. Absolutely not. I'm built of stronger stuff than that, and he's about to learn that I will cave for no one. Nope.

Screw that, I think as I take another sip of the pink stuff. *He can grovel.*

Jess disappeared on me a few minutes ago to go to the bathroom and left me to watch our glasses and hold down our table. Normally we wouldn't let each other go alone, but someone had to watch the pitcher of drinks.

"Want me to watch that for you so you can go tear his head off?" I turn my head slowly to look at Bishop, standing casually beside me in an all black suit. Black shirt, black pants, it's like he coordinated to match his hair.

"Nope. He's not worth the energy. Besides, I'm waiting for him to come over here instead. He can break first."

"He's already broken, sweetheart. But I'm almost certain that if you crooked your pretty little finger at him just so, he'd almost crawl over here for you."

I snort. "Doubtful. Cocky bastard probably doesn't know the meaning of the word."

"Try it. If you're right, I have a Benjamin in my pocket for you."

"And if you're right?"

"If I'm right, you convince your friend to let me take her out on a date. Fair?"

I look back at him. "I thought you two already were, or had…"

"No. We haven't 'dated,' as you're trying to say. But we will."

"Look at him, Ronni. He's about to crawl out of his own goddamn skin because he thinks I'm over here hitting on you. His girl. It's taking everything he has not to come over here and punch me, and all because he has some misguided notion of nobility so he'll sit over there and punish himself before he disrespects you. He would suffer before he forces himself upon you. He's just waiting for his chance to make amends and keep you."

"He had his chance before that skank showed up at his house."

"I'm not denying that. Idiot should've secured his house

better, protected you from the trauma. But the thing is, he's not in the same head space with you around. His focus is distracted. His reactions are delayed, not like before. You've seen it, right? Look at him right now."

I looked back over at him, where he's staring down Elliot and giving him an unreadable look. Or at least, a look that I couldn't decipher, but clearly Elliot did. He mouthed something at Bishop that looked like "Get the hell away from her." Bishop's head shifted slightly to the left and right in a "no" before he glanced down at me again.

"Are you two lovebirds done making moony faces at each other," I quipped.

"Do it, Veronica. Watch what happens."

"Fine," I said, resting my elbow against the tabletop and crooking my finger at Elliot once, twice, before laying my forearm down on the surface again.

To my surprise, Elliot rose from the couch, sidestepped the velvet rope with a quick fist bump at the bouncer, before stalking across the dancefloor toward me.

"Tell Jess I'll pick her up tomorrow at 7." Without another word, Bishop walks off, suspiciously in the same direction I saw Jess go earlier.

"Veronica. Can we talk for a minute?" Elliot stands in front of me with his hands in his pockets, intentionally aloof despite the stiffness in his shoulders.

"It's a free country, Moxley. You can do whatever you want." I don't dare look up from my glass, if I make eye contact with him I just know I'll crack. I'll forgive him, I'll believe whatever he says.

He sighs, and I can see him settling into the barstool beside me in my peripheral vision. He set his hands on the table, his thick fingers splaying across the wood. I can see him looking at me, but I still don't acknowledge him. My teeth clench as I smell his cologne, and feel his warmth where our forearms are almost touching.

"Ronni, can you please look at me?"

"You don't need to make eye contact with me to talk. Just talk."

"You're killing me, Snow Queen." My side eye catches him bowing his head.

My anger flares. "The feeling is mutual, Moxley. I had to listen to your ex share the short list of things you won't do in bed, and then the very, *very* long list of things that you will do happily—in detail! How am I supposed to deal with that? She could let herself into your apartment, and what did you do about it? Nothing! I had to be held hostage in your apartment by her!"

"I didn't know, I swear. I would never have left you alone like that if I knew she would get in."

"You didn't tell me about your sister, or your niece, and I had to find out after the fact. Do you not trust me? What are we even doing? I can't do this if we don't talk. If there's no way you can trust me with anything then what the hell are we even doing?"

"I can, I do, it's just," he sighs, running frustrated hands through his hair. "I don't talk about any of this to anyone. My family is off limits to the press, and everyone. It's intentional. I can't bear to have anything happen to them and I'm not willing to let them be used for publicity."

"I never wanted them for that, Elliot. I would have done what you asked, I would have left them out of the family photos and the rest of the family events that your teammates go to. It wouldn't be asking that much and I would have respected your decision wholeheartedly. You just had to tell me. You just had to trust me. And that's why," I cut off as I feel my throat tighten. "I have to go. Just show up to the list of events Jess sends you, okay?" Slowly, I turn away from him, my vision growing blurry as the tears I've held back start to fall.

"No, Ronni, wait!" His warm hand closing softly on my

hand makes me pause, and I turn back. "I'm sorry. I'm so, so sorry. Just let me try to make this up to you. We can do this and I'll communicate better, and it will be everything we talked about. Just don't walk away from me now."

Shaking my head, I turn away and feel his hand clench on mine, before slowly releasing and letting me go. He lets me walk away from him and while it is everything I needed, I still wished he would have followed.

CHAPTER 38

ELLIOT

WHOEVER SAID "distance makes the heart grow fonder" clearly never worked with their person. I can't escape her, she's everywhere. She still won't talk to me if it isn't work related, which means we spend a lot of time in short conversations with one-word answers. I think I would rather take a skate to the face than deal with this.

Jess cornered me for this field trip and I couldn't say no, even if there was a chance Ronni would be around. If I'm at least keeping my nose clean and performing the good deeds that are asked of me, I can't get in trouble. So that's how I found myself here, standing in front of a gaggle of preteens in front of the skate shop. They're all looking up at me with a mixture of emotions, ranging from boredom to adoration.

"So, this is the skate shop, where we bring our gear to be repaired between games. They make sure our skates are in good condition so we don't end up hurt or getting hauled off ice. The team also has boxes in the tunnel in case there are issues during the games. Did you guys see the game last week when Robey got hauled off the ice on one blade? They had to take his skates back here and replace the mount for his blade. They also take care of the rink girls' skates as well."

A small chorus of "oh" and "cool" come from the crowd as they shuffle by the glass walls, looking in at a worker sharpening a blade on a figure skate. As they take in their fill and start to gather around me, there's a lackluster energy about this whole thing, I know I'm feeding into it. I don't want to be here, and that's a first for me. I've always wanted to go to the arena, even when I thought I had broken my ankle and skating was sheer agony. My head and heart were not in the arena with me today.

"Now let's grab a set of skates and we'll go down the tunnel to the rink. We'll wrap up with some ice time. The equipment managers will meet us at the benches with your gear after we go and look at the locker rooms on our way there." I step back and watch the equipment team pair off with the kids to get them sized up, and just lean against the wall. Jess approaches from a side hall and freezes.

"Hey, Mox. How's the tour going?"

"Just about to wrap up, I think. We're going to make the rounds to the locker rooms, and then go to the ice. If you want some pictures, that's probably a good spot."

"Sounds good. Thanks for stepping up to the plate, I appreciate it. Bishop would have if I didn't have him double booked."

"Yeah, I know. I don't mind."

"There you are, Jess, I needed you-" Ronni's voice cuts off as she skids to a halt a few feet away. "Moxley. Hi."

"Hey Ronni – um, Ms. Snow. How are you?"

"I'm good, I think. Just busy."

"Good God, you two are ridiculous," Jess grumbles. "Ronni, go assist Mox with the rest of the tour, and then go talk or something. Seriously. This needs to stop. You both are miserable. Go figure it out."

We both look at Jess in shock. She never talks back to us, so this is surreal to hear. Before either of us open our mouths to argue, Jess is walking off and leaving us behind her.

"Well, that was…" I start to say before I realize I have no words for what that was.

"Yeah, she's never been that outspoken before. But she is getting a little short with me lately."

"I'm sorry, I shouldn't have put us in this position-"

"Now isn't the time, Mox. Get through the season first."

I bow my head, knowing she's right. When I do, I notice the boots on her feet. "Hey, aren't those the boots from when you ran me over?"

"Yeah, they are." She smiles, but it doesn't totally reach her eyes. "Johan fixed them for me."

"He's a good one. I like him fixing my equipment best."

Oh my God, this small talk is killing me.

The teens are gathering around and I'm becoming aware that they're watching us together.

"Hey, this is my friend, Ms. Ronni. She works in our Public Relations office and helped put together this little tour. How about if she tags along with us, is that cool?"

Ronni glares at me but quickly turns a bright smile toward their young faces. "Hi, have you been enjoying your behind-the-scenes tour so far?" A more enthusiastic murmur comes across for her. "So, I hear we're heading toward the locker rooms now. Has Elliot told you any of the history of the building? No? Well, did you know this wasn't the first arena for the Ice Wolves?"

Even though I am fully aware of all the history behind the building and the team, I'm completely engrossed in watching her share as she walks down the hall leading toward the visitors lockers. She drops statistics from the first game played here, and my heart clenches. Her love of the game is palpable. This is the woman who could support me through my career, no matter how long or short it may be. She is everything I've ever wanted or needed and didn't know that she was standing right here in front of me. And I blew it. I have to fix it.

We guide the group through the halls, into the visitors' locker room, point out the therapy rooms and then approach the tunnel and the door to our team locker room. The energy from the kids is palpable as they start to see areas they recognize from TV. I knock on our locker room door, peek my head in to make sure no one is in there, and then open the door the rest of the way.

"Dude, this is so cool," a short blond boy says.

"I cannot believe I'm standing here," a girl in the back whispers toward her friend.

"Oh wow, that's your spot!" Another kid called out as he walked across to look at my jersey and gear layout in front of my locker.

"Yep, they set out our fresh jerseys and gear every game, after the crew checks buckles and straps one last time. I asked for mine to be prepped early so you could see what this looks like pre-game."

"Someday, I want to have my jersey hanging in here." I looked over at a younger boy, hanging apart from the rest of the group.

"You play?" I ask?

He nods, looking over toward Bishop's nameplate. "I'm a goalie. I want to be as good as Valentin Bishop some day."

"Cool, we always need a good guy between the pipes. It can make or break a whole team. Are you coming to the training camp this summer?"

I notice his shoulder slump and darting eyes. "No, it…it doesn't work with my mom's schedule."

"Bummer. Anyone else play?" A couple hands shoot up. "And coming to camp?" The hands stay put. "Cool, cool. We like to see young blood coming through. I look forward to it every year. So, anyway, let's go down the tunnel like we do before every period, so you get the feel of it." They travel as a unit toward and out the door, except for the young goalie.

"Hey," I say softly to him. "Is there anything that'll help get you to camp?"

His eyes shoot to mine, and his cheeks glow pink. "It's–It's not working with my mom's schedule," he admits, but I can tell it's not something he enjoys talking about. "It's just really expensive for us. She works doubles to cover league fees for me."

"I understand," I say as I walk us out past Ronni. "Did you know my mom did the same thing to get me started in Mites? And then when I was older, I worked at the rink after school to get money for better gear?"

"Yeah. But I'm not old enough to do that yet. I'm going to, I don't want to give up on hockey and I love being at the rink."

"Never give up on what your heart wants, bud. Got it?" I hold out a fist to him, which he bumps with more enthusiasm. "There are some scholarships for camp, right, Ronni?"

I wink at her, and her eyes widen with recognition. "I believe you're right! Can I get your info, or your mom's email? I can send her what I know." I walk ahead, listening to him talk to Ronni and giving her his phone number. Smiling, I move toward our group milling about in the hall.

"Okay, so," I start, gaining their attention as the conversations die down. "On game day, they show us walking out of this locker room door before we emerge onto the ice before warmups and the start of the periods. You've seen this, right? Well, this is where it starts. Come on," I motion, and they fall in line behind me. Like I do every game, I tapped my knuckles on the beam that denoted the separation between the Ice Wolves support and offices, and the Theodore J. Price Arena.

I can hear the *tap-tap-tap* as they all follow suit, with a few grunts and thumps as some of the shorter kids jumped to make the tap. The view here never gets old; the darkness of the tunnel, underneath the lower bowl of seats, gives way to the glaring lights aimed at the ice, and the flashing images from the jumbotron. The voices behind me are hushed, and I can hear them point out smaller details around the oval; the organ in the right corner, the press boxes across the highest point, even the banners of retired numbers. The view from here, while visible from any other seat in the arena, just hits different from this exact point.

"Okay, everyone climb into our box here, and take a seat on the bench." I lean against the boards as I watch them shuffle in to take a seat where I instructed. When our bench is full, I guide the rest just onto the ice, across the boards in front of the announcer box, and into the visiting team bench. I step back farther on the ice in my sneakers so I can see both benches clearly. "Alright, some of the equipment team is bringing down the rental gear you had tried on before, so you can come out on the ice too. They're going to help you put on your skates and lace you up, and please stay put until we're all ready to go out at once, okay? Cool, let's do this!"

I step back inside the boards and walk down the tunnel to where Johan stood with my skates already sitting on top of the equipment repair station. I sat down on the bench beside him with a smile and started working my laces free.

"You're good at this, Elliot. You may have found your career for after your career like me," he laughs.

Johan was one of the original defensemen when the team first opened into expansion, and after retirement he never left the building. He just shifted from one side of the skate shop to the other.

"It's nothing, Johan, they're good kids. They make it easy." I toe out of my sneakers and step into my skates, lacing them up easily. "Hey, did you bring down a pair of skates for Ronni too? I know she's out there doing PR work, but I'd like to get her on the ice too."

"I'll get them down here," he replies, reaching into his pocket for his phone. After requesting Ronni's skates, he slides it back into his pocket before looking down at me. "So, you two are finally back on speaking terms?"

My hands fumble with my laces and I curse. "Nothing stays secret around here, does it?"

"My boy, you're just not good at keeping secrets," he laughs, watching me redo my laces. "Plus, you two are horrible poker players. You keep everything on your faces."

"I didn't ask to be called out like this," I grumble as I get settled on my blades. "It's rude to bust a man's balls, you know."

"I do. And that's why I'm not busting your balls, I'm telling you what I see and how to fix it. Ronni's a good girl, and you two would make an adorable hockey team together if you could get yourself figured out."

"Figuring myself out isn't the problem."

"It's not? You may want to check that. It's not bad, it's like when that shot goes wide on you. What do you do?"

"Chase the puck down, loop around, and shoot again."

"There you go."

"Are you really telling me to chase her down and shoot again? I don't know if she'll appreciate being compared to a puck."

"She'll appreciate the effort you put into it. Besides, it breaks my heart seeing her face like that. You hurt her, but you can still fix it."

"I'm working on it. Thanks for the pep talk," I say as I fist bump him and walk back to the ice. I can hear the kids talking and laughing, and the sounds of sticks tapping against the boards. "Alright, are you ready? Let's go!"

I open the door and glide out onto the ice, push the opposing bench door open, and step back as I watch all the kids take to the ice at varying speeds. Clearly, some had skating experience and shoot away from the boards. Others stayed close to the boards. I watch them all with a smile as they circled the ice. Jonah and Ronni stand behind the home bench, and Johan throws pucks onto the ice. The kids swarm the black rubber like a feeding frenzy, dribbling pucks on their sticks and taking shots at the goals. Looking back at Johan and Ronni, I skate back up to the boards.

"Come skate with me?" I ask Ronni, holding a hand out to her.

"I've never really skated before, it's probably best if I don't." I look down and see a pair of figure skates leaning on the boards by her feet, and I step into the box beside her.

"Sit down, Snow Queen. I'll help you. I won't let you fall." She freezes, her eyes bouncing between me and the skates. "I promise. You can trust me, okay?" She lowers herself to the bench, and I slowly drop to a knee in front of her.

"Are you sure this is a good idea?" She whispers, sliding the zipper down the inside of one calf. I carefully pull it off, and then hold the skate steady so she could step in.

"It may be the best idea I've had in weeks." I carefully tighten her laces for her, even though I know she's fully capable. I look up at her through my lashes, pull the loops tight, and lightly wrap my hands around her ankle. "How's that?"

"F-fine," she stutters, lowering the zipper on the other boot. "We'll see how you feel about it when you're keeping me from face planting in front of a bunch of kids."

"Keeping you from doing a header on the ice would require being really, really close to you," I murmur, as I continue working the skate on her foot. "I don't see a problem with this scenario. Do you?"

"Only that our track record being close to each other is questionable."

"It isn't that bad. I seem to remember us being really good together." I snug up the laces and tie them up. "You ready?"

CHAPTER 39

VERONICA

"YOU READY?"

He says it so calmly, like I'm not about to risk bodily damage. *I can't just go out there, I'll fall on my ass in front of people and then where will I be?* I think to myself. I can feel my heartbeat in my throat as I stand shakily on my blades on the rubber mat.

"Ready as I'm going to be, I guess," I say as I take a wobbly step in his direction.

He keeps his hands under my elbows, not grasping but just supportive, and as he steps backwards I take another step forward. And so we go until we reach the threshold where the rubber meets the ice. He steps surely backward onto the ice, sliding his hands down my forearms until my hands are resting lightly against his warm palms.

"Come on out, Ronni, I have you."

I step slowly onto the frozen surface, feeling the blade slide under my foot, and then step out with the other without letting go of his hands. He slides backwards a bit and I follow him, my eyes never leaving our hands.

"I don't know, El-"

"Look at you, you're doing just fine. Just stay with me here, okay?" I glance up and around, and realize that we've now skated out and around to the opposing goal. "We're going to turn, and go behind the net. Then, if you're feeling good with that, I'll let go of one hand. If you fall I'll catch you."

"Okay."

Just as he describes, he lets go with one hand and watches, at the ready. It's not as hard as I thought it was, and soon I feel the surrounding breeze while we make another lap around the rink, nearly oblivious to the chaos around us as the kids break into scrimmages on either end.

"Great, you're doing so good," he praises, and I look up at him with a smile when—

"Look out!" I hear behind us. Before I can turn to look, Elliot has me wrapped in his arms and we're pressed against the glass, just in time for someone to run into his back. "Sorry, guys!"

"It's cool," Elliot says, turning his head to look back at whoever ran into us. "You good?" I hear an affirmative answer and then a chorus of apologies, before he turns back to me. "Are you alright?" His breath skates along my ear, moving the loose hair from my ponytail. I look down and realize that he has me cocooned between his arms, his hands on the plexiglass behind me. I have a death grip on his hoodie.

"Yeah, I'm good. I didn't even see them coming. Thanks for the save."

"Anytime."

"Um, Moxley?"

"Yeah?"

"I think you can move now," I say with a nervous laugh.

He looks down, shock on his face. "Oh, yeah, I guess so." Slowly, he skates back from me and watches as I tentatively shift on my skates away from the boards. As I get my footing under me, he again shifts beside me. "There you go. Looks like the Snow Queen belongs on ice after all."

"Oh hush, I look like a baby deer out here."

He chuckles and skates in front of me, twisting to skate backward while facing me. "You're not that bad. Keep going."

"I question your ability to judge what's good, Mox," I laugh. "But this is kind of fun, I think I get why you like this."

"This is just part of the fun," I counter, as we come past the bench. "You should try shooting a puck." Reaching over the boards, he pull a stick out and hands it to me.

"I shouldn't be trusted with this. I'm not ready to do anything except stay upright." I bite my bottom lip, the nerves fluttering in my belly as I look around the rink at the kids practicing their skating and puck handling skills. "I should get back to the office anyway and let you get back to it." I slowly inch toward the bench, and the doorway to the locker room. "Thanks for this, Mox, it was fun."

Before I can lose my nerve, I step onto the rubber matting and head toward the chair with my shoes. Don't look back, I tell myself over and over as I sit down to unlace the skates.

"Ronni, wait," he calls after me, and I can hear him approaching. "Hold on, let me help you."

"You don't have to-"

"Ronni. Please. Let me help you. You can still leave if you want to, I won't make you stay, but just," he sighs, looking up at me from his knees. "Just let me do this one thing that I can get right for you, okay?"

"Oh, Elliot," I murmur, guilt tightening in my gut. You can get a lot of things right, you have gotten a lot of things right before.

"Just not us."

"Just not us," I confirm. "Maybe the timing was all wrong. Maybe it just wasn't meant to be."

"I still want to fix it, Veronica, and I swear I'm going to make this better."

"You need to focus on your game, and stay out of trouble for the rest of the season. Priorities."

"I know." He rests his hands on my ankles, now out of the protection of the skates and secured in my boots.

"Later, El," I whisper as I move to stand, sliding my hand along his messy strands. He keeps his head bowed as I walked away.

"Later, Snow Queen," I hear him softly reply, and with each step I could have sworn I felt my heart break again.

CHAPTER 40

ELLIOT

I KEPT MY PROMISE, and I didn't chase after Ronni that afternoon at the rink. I dropped a line through Jess to make sure she made it back to the PR offices and then I kept my distance for the week. The ball was coming, and with it came the auction. I knew both women would be busy with the preparations, so I didn't track them down to run my idea past them until the last minute.

I watch from the cracked double doors as they both work seamlessly together, rearranging the table settings and the display tables for the auction. Uniform tablecloths, in our trademarked teal and silver, pressed and pleated. Their attention to detail was impeccable, and the ballroom looked amazing.

"Jess, do you have more of that double-stick tape? I need more over here for the helmet displays."

Jess walked over to her, pulling out a roll and handing it to Ronni where she looked at a table with five platform squares, just the right size to hold helmets.

Ronni tore off small pieces and placed them under the smaller silver clothes over the platforms, artfully arranging them.

"We need easels between these tables," Jess motioned to the long tables beside her.

"Michael is coordinating with maintenance to get them over here," Ronni confirmed.

I felt bad for just watching them work, so I snuck inside the space, leaning against the wall. "Do you ladies need any help setting up?"

Jess's eyebrows shoot up in surprise as she sees me standing inside the door, my hands in my pockets.

"Hey, Moxley!" Jess's voice is friendly, but it isn't the one I want to hear. *Please*, I mentally beg, *talk to me, Snow Queen.*

"Um, I'm going to go see if Michael has an update on the easels. See ya, Ronni! Hi, bye, Moxley!" She bolts for the door before either of us could argue the point with her. The doors clicked shut behind her, and that was it. We were alone for the first time in weeks.

"I think I'm good, but thanks, Moxley."

"Ronni, I-"

"Please. It's Veronica." I sigh and cringe at her terse tone, as well as the full first name. "Look, I know you mean well, but I just," she pauses, swallowing hard, "I can't do this with you right now, I just can't." Her eyes dart away from me, and if I didn't know better, I'd think I saw tears.

"I'm so sorry, I just want to make it better. I want us to go back to the way things were before." I walk up to her slowly, giving her a chance to back away. I get close enough to be just inside her personal space, but not so close as to look improper. "Baby, please. Talk to me." She nods her head, but still won't make eye contact with me. "I want to fix this for us. I'll do anything to make it better." I can't help my hand coming between us, cupping the side of her face, and catching the rogue tear dangling precariously from her lashes with my thumb. "I hate that I'm making you cry."

"I suppose I'm asking too much for you to not make me cry, aren't I?" The words came out watery, and I watch helplessly as she sucks her bottom lip in between her teeth. "I should've known better. It was too good to be true."

"Don't do that," I begged her. "Don't downplay us. We were good before, and we can be good again, just promise me we can try again."

Her eyes drop closed, wet eyelashes glittering. "We can talk about it after the season ends. You need to concentrate and stay out of trouble."

"I miss you, you know," I murmur at her, wondering how hard she'd smack me if I pulled her closer to me.

"I know. I miss you too. It just hurts to see you every day." She smiles lightly. "It's hard to avoid you around here, and it's even harder when you get a suspension."

I chuckle, throwing caution to the wind and stepping into her, sliding my hand around her hip. I mentally celebrate this small victory and leaned closer, resting my forehead against hers.

"I don't know if I'm supposed to be sorry about that."

"You're not sorry at all, you have this wild way of staying in trouble. It's like you do it on purpose." She shifted in my arms, her own wrapping around my waist.

"Well, is it working?"

"Elliot." Her tone had a note of warning to it. "Can you ever just be serious for a moment?"

"Sometimes. It's not as fun to be serious, though."

"Seriousness is what keeps me employed, though." Her head tilts to look up at me. "Do you know that Lacey has been calling Michael's office about me?"

I freeze. "No. Why didn't you say anything?"

She bows her head, cheeks pink. "I was angry, embarrassed, I didn't want to see you or hear your voice, so I didn't want to hear you say you'd fix it. I definitely didn't want to know how you'd fix it." She heaves a sigh. "So far he's blowing her off because he knows this is just retaliation from the press work we did to fix the mess from the offseason. But

I can't depend on that forever. If she can get a hold of upstairs, I don't know what will happen to me. To you."

I feel the vein in my temple throb. "I'm going to fix this, Ronni, I swear. She can't do this to you, none of this is your fault! I'm go to-"

"You're going to sit down with your teammates at the ball tomorrow night and act like everything is lovely. No fighting, no public statements, no antagonizing your ex. Got it?"

"But-"

"No buts, just do this, okay?"

She stares me down harder than anyone ever had previously in a face-off with me. I can't argue with her, I know she's right. Even if I wanted to fight for her, I know she doesn't want that. I know I needed to respect her boundaries on this, but I also don't want her shouldering all the weight.

"Okay, I will. How are the donations coming together?"

"Not bad. There's some signed gear from the guys. Bishop apparently threatened everyone with 'death by burpees' if they didn't produce something."

"Can neither confirm nor deny. I threw my name on the team jersey after practice."

"I appreciate that. Every bit helps."

"I heard there are still some last-minute deliveries coming though. I have hope that this will be the best year ever for the foundation."

Her eyes scanned the room, her cheeks glowing red. "I hope so too. Jess has really put a lot into it." She looks up into my face. "Thanks for coming to help, and for just being here."

"Did you need a ride tomorrow or anything? I can come get you and save you the cab."

"We're just coming in the same car, not as your date, right?"

"It's only as big or small as you want it to be. I'd love to come in with you on my arm, for everyone to know you're my girl, but I won't push the issue."

She popped onto her toes and placed a soft kiss against my cheek. "Let's just start as carpool buddies and see where we go from there."

"I can do that." We may not have gotten through everything, but it was a step in the right direction.

CHAPTER 41

VERONICA

MY GUT IS IN KNOTS. I've been here for an hour already, watching the caterers bustle around stocking the drink stations in the corners, and the deejay setting up his station in the larger ballroom for the dancing. We have laid the auction items out in the entry, Jess had managed that portion herself. I stood in the middle of the main room, taking in the surrounding chaos, willing myself not to clench the pale blue satin wrapped around me for fear of it wrinkling. I itched to do something–anything–to keep myself busy, and avoid dwelling on the stress of the upcoming event. We had planned everything out to the finest detail, everything should be fine, but I couldn't help but worry.

"Ronni, this looks fantastic!" Michael's voice boomed from across the hall at me. I smiled at him, gathering my long skirts, I made my way over to him.

"Thank you, Jess really knocked this one out of the park!"

"Where is she? I need to tell her this as well."

"She should be in the next room putting the finishing touches on the auction displays and completing checks with the security team. Let's go, I'll take you in," I reply, motioning toward the doorway beside us. "She had a whole thing planned. When the doors open for the guests, they will have to walk through the displays on the way into the dinner. They can't miss it."

Together we pass through the door into the entryway, watching the security lining the hall, Jess standing in the middle in a jade green dress. She grins and waves at us before turning her attention back to the clipboard wielding assistant beside her.

"Great job, Jess, you've really outdone yourself! This looks bigger and better than last year!" Michael's voice booms in the open space as he approaches.

"Thanks, Michael, I appreciate it. I couldn't have done it without you two for sure. We really make a great team."

"Well, I hope we can stay this way for a few years now," he replied. "Good help is so hard to find sometimes." After a few more final checks, we head to open the doors for the red carpet.

Outside, the press had set up to take photos of the incoming players and foundation guests invited to the event. I watched as some of the younger, newer players arrived early, and greeted everyone as they arrived while Jess gave more instructions inside. Everyone paused in front of the team banner and posed, either solo or as a couple. As the more well-known players came I directed them inside and reminded the press that we would not be fielding questions today outside of what label they were wearing.

Robicheaux, decked in a bright blue tux, flashed smiles as cameras clicked. "Ronni, *mon ami*, come and take your picture with me!"

"Robey, just do your thing so you can go inside, you're holding up the line!" Bishop yelled from where he had just climbed out of the SUV. He smoothed out the wrinkles on his black on black outfit as he waited.

"Come on, Robey." I waved him over toward the door so he could go inside.

"Come on, Ronni" he responded in a joking tone, *"Une seule photo s'il vous plaît!"*

I gave him a look that said let's go, and he responded by giving me begging praying hands.

"Fine, just one. And don't you dare get it in your head that I only responded because you spoke French," I grumbled, walking over to the tape X he stood near.

Plastering what I hoped was a realistic smile on my face, I stood close enough that he could wrap an arm around me for the photo, then, stepped back. "Better now? Get inside, Jess is going to have your head."

"Yeah, I know, and so is that man of yours. He said the first one to touch you does stingers in practice Monday until they puke."

"That's horrifying," I said in shock, before stepping away from him. "Hurry, get inside."

"Too late, Mox is behind me," Bishop said from beside us.

"It's okay, you're worth it," Robicheaux laughs as he walked away.

"Oh my God, you boys are ridiculous," I groan as I start to walk away.

"No, you don't, get back over here," Bishop calls before I take two steps. "I'm not letting that little punk upstage me, and Mox won't make me do a damn thing. You're getting in here, too."

"You're killing me, seriously?" I again walk over, smile and pose, and then direct Bishop inside. "There, done. Who's in line next–oh, hey, Mox."

CHAPTER 42

ELLIOT

MY TEAMMATES ARE ASSHOLES, I grumble to myself as Robey and then Bishop stand there, pulling my girl in close, and get their picture taken on the red carpet with her. The red carpet event I wanted to attend with her. Hell, they got the pictures that I wanted, and they knew it. Moral of the story? Never tell your teammates that you're hot for a girl.

So I stand here in line, waiting my turn to go stand on the little black X they had marked out for us in front of the photographers, and contemplate all the ways I could make them suffer. It would be glorious.

"I suppose you'll want me up here too," Ronni asks softly, looking up at me.

Without saying a word, I grab her hand, pulling her closer to me than she stood with my friends, and slide my other arm around her. It's a possessive pose; I know it. Her gasp is music to my ears, and I enjoy the way her hand comes up to rest on my chest, her skirt whipping around my leg as she steps into my hold. I look down at her, her eyes locked on mine as she bites her bottom lip. I wink at her before turning my face back toward the cameras, flashing that megawatt smile I'm known for. Photos done, I allow my hand at her waist to relax and drop away.

"See you later, Snow Queen," I whisper as I head into the venue. Shit, she's going to kill me for that one.

The murmuring in the hall as fans and benefactors gather around the tables is an annoying hum in my ears as I wander to find Bishop and Jess. I know where one is, the other won't be far behind. I don't know what happened to them but it feels like they have a lot of unresolved tension whenever they're in the same room.

I find them in a corner, standing by a mannequin holding game-worn pieces that Bishop had signed. Jess stands before him facing away from me, arms crossed in front of her chest, feet braced wide, like she's prepared for a fight. Her long red ponytail danced down her back; whatever she was saying was definitely animated. Bishop just looked down at her, that one eyebrow of his raised, and his eyes never wavering from her. I continue to walk over to them, thinking that he would see me coming before I could get in earshot, but he jolted when I said his name.

"Bishop, can I borrow Jess for a second?"

She whips around to look at me with enough force that her hair whipped Bishop's thick arm. Her eyes go wide, and I flinch, thinking that the fight and fire I saw would be unleashed on me, before her expression softens into her professional smile.

"What can I do for you, Moxley?" Her question is pleasantly worded, professional and welcoming, but her hands are still clenched at her sides.

Man, is she pissed at him or what, I think. "I have a last-minute entry into the events list. It's really important."

She clenches her jaw lightly before the smile returns. "What kind of last-minute entry are you thinking?"

"Well, I'm hoping it's one that Ronni will appreciate, and hopefully not kill me over. I want to put my Lemieux jersey in the lineup for the Children's Cancer Fund of the foundation. I also have a small statement to go with it, if that's okay." I pull the small stack of index cards from the inside pocket of my jacket and hold them out for her. "I don't even need to do them in person. I just," I suck in a breath, "She told me I needed to be more open about things in my life, and that not everyone around me would use my name or my family for a meal ticket. This is important to me, and I've given in the past anonymously; this time, I'm doing it to make a point."

She shoots a few looks between me and the cards in her hands as she scans through them, and I know when she reads it was my first big purchase with my first pro payday; her incredulous look tells me it wasn't as meaningful of an investment as I thought it was my rookie year. Her mouth drops open in shock when she gets to the card with Gabby's story on it, and I watch her face crumple as she reads through it.

"Oh, Elliot, I'm so sorry," she sniffs. "I had no idea how involved you are with her care."

"She's in an okay spot now, but I may have caused some issues with Ronni by not being open about it from the start, and that was on me. This may not fix us, but I can at least take the step toward doing better."

"That's big of you, Mox," Bishop says from her side, reaching out to give me a supportive slap on the arm. "You didn't have to do that, and I know what Gabby and the jersey mean to you. Are you positive about this?"

"Yeah, I am." I smile at them, nodding in confirmation. "The jersey may have been the most important thing in my life at the time, but things have changed some since then. This will help more."

"So, where is this jersey? We'll need to move fast if we're going to get this situated in time for the auction," Jess says, looking at her phone. "For the next few minutes, Ronni will be busy settling the Board of Trustees at their tables before dinner service, and speaking with them. She won't know I'm gone yet."

"Or," Bishop starts, "You take care of everything here. We'll go get the jersey and meet up with you." She dips her head in agreement and then. Jess walks away from us, and I motion for Bishop to come toward the opposite hallway.

"I dropped it off here earlier" I mention casually as I walked over toward a utility closet.

"You left a $5,000 signed and authenticated jersey sitting in a utility closet? Boy, you have lost your head, haven't you?"

"It isn't that serious," I say, rolling my eyes at him as I pull out a key from my pocket. "I know a guy here, he let me in."

Opening the closet, I carefully pull out the shadow box frame that previously hung in my living room, next to my college championship finals jersey. I stroke my fingers across the wood frame one last time, smooth out the black cloth I covered it in, and hand it out to Bishop.

"You know you could've kept the jersey and just donated the money, right? You've made your point."

"No, I need to do this." I lock the door behind me and walked back out in front of Bishop, who had the frame in his firm grasp. I didn't dare look at it or touch it again; I didn't want to risk losing my nerve. "Okay, texting Jess." I peek around a corner at most the crowd, and see where Jess has brought out another easel like the signed posters had stood on. I motion for Bishop to follow to the easel, where we carefully set the item, and then nonchalantly walk toward the main event hall as if nothing had happened. We entered the space together, Bishop and I both stopping for a drink from the bartender and scanning the crowd, waving at a few familiar faces. Nonchalance was key. We didn't just do anything.

Jess approaches as we search for our seating assignments. "Are you boys done?"

"We are," I confirm with a nod. "Thanks for the setup."

"Let's not make a habit of this, okay?" She stretches a hand out, pointing toward a table to the right. "Moxley, I have you at this table. You'll be seated with the donor coordinator for the Children's Cancer Fund, so expect a photo op or handshake when the auction is announced."

"Thanks for everything Jess, I'm just going to head that direction. Hey, where's Bishop going?"

"Bishop is sitting over here, with a couple rookies, the commissioner, and Ronni. Commissioner's choice."

Bishop and I both glanced at each other, wondering what the plan was there. He shrugs at me and wanders over toward the table, shaking the commissioner's hand before approaching his seat.

Ronni approaches as he rounded the table, and he holds out a chair for her to sit in after she greets their table mates. It feels like a punch to the gut, watching him take care of her the way I wanted.

"Come on, Moxley, she's in good hands." Jess's statement is soft, only in my ear, and her small hand against by back nudges me into motion.

"Bishop's going to be pissed if he sees that," I murmur as we walked toward my table.

"He'll get over it. I'm not his property."

Looking backward, I lock eyes with Bishop and nod toward Ronni. Unspoken communication, much like we do on ice, pass between us. He would take care of her, if I took care of Jess. With that agreed upon, I followed Jess over to the table, and hold her chair out.

This is going to be a long night, I grumble in my head as I sit down with my professional smile firmly in place.

CHAPTER 43

I WATCH Jess direct Moxley to his table, and the backwards glances he keeps sneaking to me. I did it on purpose, placing myself at the commissioner's table with Bishop instead of at his table, and Jess sitting with him, make sure he behaved, and everything would be fine.

"Everything okay, Snow?" Bishop leans over toward me, keeping our words between us and away from the rookies.

"It'll be fine."

"You look as nervous as a long-tailed cat in a room of rocking chairs, relax a bit." I shoot him a look as he picks up his rocks glass of scotch and sips the amber liquid thoughtfully. "Jess is going to keep him in line, you know that, right?"

"I know." I reach over for my water glass, hoping that the surrounding conversations would cover up the rattling of my ice cubes. I'm not cool with my nerves on stark relief like that.

The commissioner asks Bishop a question about the upcoming playoffs, and I allow the conversation between the men to distract me as the dinner continues. Occasionally I'm drawn into the discussion, with potential ideas for golf tournaments in the offseason and future benefit galas. As we finish the dinner portion of the evening, I excuse myself to go up and continue the next major portion of the event; awards, and the auction.

I take my place at the podium, Jess coming up beside me, and we introduce the board members and players, before inviting the commissioner up for some remarks. We listen politely as he speaks on how important the foundation and its charity wings are to the community, and how there were hopes that this would be another fabulous year. Jess and I bring forward the items, one at a time. Bidding wars break out, and before we know it, there are only two items left; Bishop's stick from the last game, and the jersey signed by everyone.

The commissioner calls Bishop up to pick up the stick and then start the bidding while he displays it. I steal a glance over at Jess, whose eyes glow with pride as she looks on at the large man. I have hopes for them; even if things were rocky with Elliot and I, it would have been cool if one relationship left the season unscathed.

The final bid was declared on Bishop's stick, so I reach over for the jersey that was signed by all the players, and encased in a shadow box with a team photo. I pause, looking at the easels. I can see the jersey, but there's another easel covered in a black cloth beside it.

"Jess? What's that?" I point toward it, confusion pinching my brow. I know we accounted for everything beforehand.

"Shh, don't worry about that one yet." She steps over to me and helps to move the team jersey onto the stage by the podium and then motion for me to walk back toward my table.

"We have an extra. There isn't supposed to be an extra!" I hiss at her between my smiling teeth as we approach my chair. Bishop stands by, pulling my chair back out for me.

"Just wait. You'll see, I promise. Bishop, get her a glass of wine, please? Thank you."

The auction continues, and I maintain my internal panic

behind my smile. Clearly something was up and I just didn't know what. The jersey, as we predicted, sold for an unheard of total, exceeding last year's winning bid. A loud round of applause erupts as the jersey is taken from the easel.

The commissioner looks over toward Elliot's table. "I have it on good authority that there is one more late submission, with a personal delivery from our own captain, Elliot Moxley." Polite applause breaks out, and Elliot makes his way up to the podium. With a handshake between the two, and a supportive arm-clap from the commissioner, they swap places. Elliot pulls out a small stack of index cards from his inside pocket, and I watch him take a calming breath; it's a movement I've watched him do countless times in press conferences.

"Hi everyone. Thanks for letting me take some time here. I had something important that I wanted to give and of course I needed to take too long to figure out what to do about it." The crowd laughs, and he continues, "You see, I know a great girl who showed me that not everything is negative. I've had a secret that no one knows about me. My agent may freak out, because I had him swear never to talk about this. I have a niece who is a patient in the oncology wing that The Ice Wolves Foundation supports, and for that, I will always be grateful." A series of *aww*'s peppered the crowd. "I've tried to keep her out of the media, and in the process I may have abused the trust of my friends; I trust them on ice, and with my public image, but for some reason not with this. I felt like I needed to make a change and do my part, and so here I am."

My mouth drops open in horror. "Oh my God, what is he-"

"Shhh." Bishop cuts me off with a sharp look and a nod toward Elliot. I look back over at him, his eyes drifting toward me for a second, before he goes back to his speech.

"So, today, I'm making a donation of my own." He walks over to the black cloth, removing it, revealing his most prized possession. "Everyone knows that Mario Lemieux is one of my idols. What few people know is that my first major purchase with my first pro contract was this jersey. If my house ever caught on fire, this would be what I'd run in for, as long as everyone living was out," he chuckles, and the crowd joins in. "The thing is, Gabby also means the world to me. That's why I am putting this jersey up for auction, with the proceeds going specifically to the Ice Wolves Children's Cancer Fund, and I will match the bid amount dollar for dollar, in her name, besides $10,000 on my own." I gasp aloud, as did a majority of the crowd. That was insanity. "If you've never had the pleasure of meeting or working with the Children's Cancer Fund or the oncology team through the University Cancer Center, you're missing out. These people are phenomenal and really deserve a round of applause. Some of them are here tonight, actually." He pauses while the guests all applaud.

"I can't let him do that, Bishop, he loves-" His meaty hand lands on mine where I tried to push away from the table. My eyes dart from his hand to his face.

"Let the man speak, okay?"

"There's another person who made this all possible, but doesn't really know it. I'm sure many of you have met Jess and Ronni previously, they are the ones who put together this whole event for us. They did a great job, right?" I look over at Jess trying to figure out where exactly he was going with all of this. "What some of you don't know is that for the whole season, Ronni has been the one keeping me in line, setting up the events, straightening up the press, and she's been my backbone, even when I thought I was a screwup. I don't think I would be here without her. Actually, no. I know I wouldn't be here without her. I would've been shipped off to some farm team far away from here, and still trying to learn my lesson." I giggle, he wasn't too far off base there. "In all actuality, there were times where I felt like she'd pack me up and ship me off herself, rather than deal with my antics," he laughs, looking at me, "but she just fought me harder until she got her way. And I really, really cannot thank her enough for that. You're one of a kind, Snow Queen." My heart stutters in my chest as we make eye contact, and he winks at me. "Now, let's get down to business. Commish, can you start the bidding, please?"

CHAPTER 44

ELLIOT

THE COMMISSIONER APPROACHES me at the podium, and I shake his hand before turning to walk back to my table, smiling at Jess off to the side. She gives me a thumbs up and then looks back toward Ronni, who looks stunned into silence at what I've done. It's okay, I feel better now. Sure, I have an empty spot on my wall that needs refilling, but it's okay.

A few of my teammates high-five me as I walk toward the table, and the cancer fund director shakes my hand as I move to sit down. I feel my phone ringing in my pocket, so I excuse myself and walked out into the hall while the auction battles on. I look at the screen and jump when I see Sami's name. She knows where I am tonight, so she would only call if it was a real emergency.

"Sami?"

"El, It's Gabs. They found a match. I," she pauses, "I need to go to Vegas. Now."

"Vegas? Why?" She sounds so insistent, I don't want to dissuade her from going, but I need to know.

"Because," she sighs in that way she did when she really

didn't want to say what the truth was, "because that's where her dad lives."

I freeze. "What do mean, 'that's where her dad lives.' You said you didn't know who he was."

"I didn't say I didn't know. I just didn't want to acknowledge him."

"Sami, I don't understand-"

"Just," she sniffs. Great, she's crying, and alone, and she needs me. "Can you just come over here and stay with Gabs? She knows I need to leave, she just doesn't really know the details. I'll tell her when I get back, and you as well. Everything, I promise."

"You know I will, Samsquatch. Give me a second to get out of this monkey suit and I'll be right there, okay? Do you need a ride to the airport?"

"No, I'll take a taxi. Just give me a shout when you're on your way."

We say our goodbyes, and I drop a quick text to Bishop letting him know what was going on. I barely caught the loud "Sold!" and the crack of a gavel passing through the door of the ballroom as I head to the exit, roaring applause in my wake.

I run home long enough to change into warm-up pants and an Ice Wolves t-shirt, gather an overnight bag, and then go over to Sami and Gabby's place. I walk in the door as quietly as I can, so I wouldn't wake Gabby, and step carefully into the living room, narrowly avoiding the large suitcase in the doorway.

"Jeez, Sami, are you moving there?"

"No. I don't know how long this is going to take. I'm not leaving until I have this fixed."

"Have you talked to whoever this is? I mean, does he know you're coming, or anything? What's your plan?"

"I don't really have one." She drops bonelessly onto the couch, as if saying the words suddenly made it far too heavy and real. "I just know that if I'm standing there, face to face, he won't say no. He can't say no, anyway."

"I really don't like this idea, Sami, I'm serious." I drop onto the couch beside her. "I'm worried about your safety over there by yourself. I respected your privacy before when you didn't want to say who the father was, but what if you go missing? Where do I send the cops?"

"Look, El, I know you want to big brother the shit out of me about this, but this needs to happen for Gabby. I'll send you the flight info and my hotel reservation. I'm going to try to get in and out before her next appointment next week, okay?"

"Okay, I'll trust you. But if you need anything—anything at all—you call me. I'll get on the next plane and leave Gabby with Bishop."

"Promise. Thanks, El," she says while throwing her arms around me. "Okay, that should be my ride," she adds as her phone chirped in her pocket.

"Be safe. Love you."

"Love you too." She pops a kiss on my cheek and heads toward the door. I gather her bags and follow her to the car, loading the trunk, and then watching the car pull away. As the taillights fade away in the night, I wonder exactly what she was up to.

Either way, I have a girl upstairs to entertain for a few days and I think this was just the distraction I needed.

I pull my phone out and check my texts with Bishop. He had sent back a confirmation that he knew where I had gone, but the new message notification tally spoke to far more than that. Twenty unread messages from one particular number: Snow Queen.

What are you doing??

No, really. WTF ARE YOU DOING??

You can't do that. You love that thing!

You don't have to do this to prove something to me, you know. I get it. I do.

So help me God, I'm going to strangle you when I see you.

Fine. I'll take care of this then. Where are you?

Goddamnit Moxley! Where. The Fuck. Are you?

I couldn't help but grin. She's gorgeous when she gets fired up about something, and clearly this did it. Guilt twists in my gut a little. I could have told her about the plan, and the program I discussed with the director of the cancer fund, but this was something I needed to do for myself, for my family. She would understand in time, I'm sure. With a grin, I dial her number. I know the benefit was wrapping up.

"You'd better be calling me to say you were hit by a truck." Her delivery was almost cordial, but I could still feel the ice in her words.

"What if I wasn't hit by a truck?"

"I'll hunt you down and do it myself then. Where the hell are you? You drop a surprise auction on us and bounce? That's not cool, even if it was for an amazing cause!"

"I'm sorry, Snow Queen. It won't happen again, promise. How did it go?"

"Better than anyone probably expected. Hope your checkbook is ready, that bid match is going to hurt you a bit."

"It's worth it," I chuckle. "So I wanted to ask, did Bishop say anything to you?"

"He said you had a good excuse for leaving early and I shouldn't kill you, but I'm undecided. You'll have to convince me. Are you okay though? Why did you leave?"

"Sami and Gabby needed me. Kind of connected to why I called, I'm going to be out of commission for the next week or so. I'm watching Gabby while Sami goes out of town on an emergency trip. Can you rearrange my schedule some, pretty please?"

"Of course I can. Do they need any help? Anything I can do for them?"

"I love your heart, Snow Queen, but I think we're okay. Gabs and I are just going to hang at her house in between appointments. It's easier to manage her care here than at my place. She has her stuff and her own bed, and can rest better."

"Don't you have practice and things still? I can come in and help during practice."

"Actually, that might be great. If she's up for the trip, I might bring her in but she gets bored watching alone. She'd love to see you again."

"I'd love to hang with her again, too." I could hear the smile in her voice as she answered. "So, are you going to tell me why you didn't let me know what your plan was today?"

"I didn't want you to think it was just for you. It wasn't. Not really. Shit, that sounds like a dick statement to say. I mean-"

"You mean you didn't want me thinking it was all a ploy to get me back. I get it. It just threw me off because we had the whole night planned to the minute."

"I'm sorry. Did it make the commissioner happy?"

"You know it," she laughs. "You set a record, and I'm pretty sure players for years are going to be wondering how to break this record."

"I'll give them lessons and threaten them within an inch of their lives if they surprise you again."

"Thank you. I fucking hate surprises."

"I swear, the only surprises I'll give you from now on are good ones."

CHAPTER 45

VERONICA

I HAVE A HUGE SECRET, and it's killing me. I'm not big on secrets anyway, surprises even more so than that. This, however, is the biggest of both. I can't tell anyone, not even Jess.

Elliot's prized possession, his favorite jersey, is sitting in my living room.

Bishop, seeing my panic as the bidding war launched and I couldn't stop it, slipped me an important piece of paper under my napkin and said go wild. A blank check, paid from his personal account. Of course I couldn't just jump into the war blindly. I almost backed out as the number jumped higher, but his steady voice beside me kept me in it. He couldn't bid outright, but he also couldn't let his best friend's prized possession go to someone else either. So, with his backing and my bidding, we saved it. It was delivered this morning, and no one was the wiser. However, I couldn't keep it a secret forever and it was honestly killing me to not say anything.

I tried to get in touch with Elliot this morning but he didn't answer. I tried to get in touch with Bishop to see if he had keys to Elliot's place so we could put it back where it came from, and he agreed to meet me there later in the day. So now, here I was, sneaking over to Elliot's apartment to put it back. Bishop is supposed to be already upstairs.

The doorman kindly helped me with the frame to the hallway, where I tipped him and then pulled out my phone to call Bishop after he didn't answer the door. I didn't get an answer on his phone, so I waited. And waited. I didn't want to haul this back downstairs, and I didn't feel comfortable just leaving it here in the hallway either. In a moment of boredom, I sat and leaned my head against the door, getting comfortable so I could scroll the social media posts on my phone. Throwing some posts on the schedule killed some time, and then I dropped another text to Bishop to ask how much longer he would be. It was at that moment that the door opened on me, allowing my head to fall backward, bouncing off of the tile floor and leaving me to look up at a very confused, damp, and slightly angry Elliot.

"Ronni? Oh my God, are you okay? What are you doing here?" He bends down, his sopping wet hair dripping down on me, grasping my arms to get me upright again.

"I think the real question is what are you doing here? You're not supposed to be here."

"It's my apartment, who else did you expect to be here?"

Shit. Shit shit shit. I can't tell him the truth but I also can't leave the jersey outside, or take it back home.

"Um," I take a deep breath, gaining some confidence. "Bishop is supposed to be meeting me here."

"Bishop was just here a few minutes before I got in the shower, he didn't say you were coming by."

"Well, the thing is, or was, I didn't want you here when I got here. Shit, that's not what it sounded like. I mean, I wanted to surprise you."

He stares at me, his forehead creased. "I don't think I understand."

"One second." I reach outside the door, grabbing the box

with the frame in it. "I wanted to get this in and back where it belonged before you got home."

His eyes bounce like ping pong balls from me to the box, back again, before bouncing to the empty spot on the wall that I could see from the entryway.

"Ronni," he breathed. "Oh, baby, what did you do?"

"Before you say anything, it wasn't just me. Okay? I couldn't have done this alone." His eyes locked on the box as I pause. "I'll let the other party tell you about it if they're comfortable with it."

"Fine," he nods. "But please tell me that isn't what I think it is in that box. My heart can't take it."

"Just open it, Mox, okay?"

He picks up the box as though it weighed nothing, and carries it into the dining room, laying it across the glossy surface. Picking up a knife from one of the place settings, he carefully cut the tape open before prying open the lid.

"It's not, it can't be, can it?" With shaking hands, he pulls back the wrapping, revealing the glass front with the jersey he loved inside. "Oh, Ronni, babe, I-"

"You didn't need to do that. We knew why you did it and couldn't bear to see you without it."

He crumples into a chair, his face dropping into his hands. "I never thought...Oh wow, I'm just," he trailed off as his wide eyes turn to me. "Come here, please, I just need..."

I walk closer to him, close enough that he could engulf one of my hands in his and pull me closer to him, I stumble, falling into his lap where he immediately wrapped me in a hug, Not a sexual gesture, just one of comfort. His head burrows on my shoulder, and I just hold him back, running my fingers through his cold hair. I could hear him whispering something against my shirt, but I couldn't make out the words.

"What? I can't hear you."

"That explains a lot, actually. Like why Bishop told me I

had better get ready. I thought he was just coming to bust my balls, earlier. But he said I needed to get ready because my life was getting ready to change."

"He's really turning into Yoda in his old age. He told me something similar during the auction."

"You don't think he-"

"-no, he wouldn't, would he?"

Our phones ding simultaneously, mine from the doorway where I dropped it, his from the hall table. I get up from his lap, going over to my phone before turning to him where he had gone to get his. We flip our screens face up, to see matching "Bishop" notifications.

"What did he do?" We say at the same time before flipping the message open.

> Bishop: I swear to fucking God if you two don't get fucking married after this, I'm locking you in a closet together until you do. Stupid kids don't know stupid love when it trips them. You've been dancing around this for the whole damn season. Sack up and do it. Apologize, have wild make up sex, and quit being miserable shits.

> Bishop: PS, I'm taking Gabby out for ice cream and pizza until she hurls, and all the scary movies she wants, and then staying up past her bedtime. You can't stop me. As honorary uncle, this is my right.

I laugh at the message before looking over at Elliot, who is decidedly not laughing.

"Elliot?" He looks at me. "He's just kidding, right?" His eyes drift shut and with a muttered curse, he's pocketing his phone. "Right?"

"Sure. We weren't ready for that yet, anyway."

My heart starts racing. "What are you talking about?"

"It's stupid, don't worry about it."

"You look like he just shot your dog, El. What's wrong?"

He looks back at me. "If I tell you, you can't get mad at me, okay? And I'm not saying it has to happen now. Just," he groans, "it was all wishful thinking and then Lacey happened, and I just put it to the back of my mind. He, however, doesn't forget a damn thing."

"Okay, just tell me."

"It's better if I show you." He walks into the hallway, heading toward the office that he had set up.

Sitting on the couch was a big white box with the team colors in a big ribbon. "Now, I just want you to know this has been here since before you left last time. It's been here the whole time. Open it."

I look at him, his nervous posture completely out of character for the overly confident player that I knew. With shaking hands, I reach out to the box, Carefully removing the lid, I pull back the layers of tissue paper to find a team jersey, with a simple black box centered on the patch.

"Elliot, is this…," the words escaped me. He steps forward slowly, reaching down to pick up the box.

"I had very specific plans for this, but the timing was never right. And that's okay, because we still had a lot to learn about each other. When the time is right, I hope we can circle back to this one."

"What's in the box, Elliot?"

"I'll show it to you when we're ready. Until then, I think the jersey speaks for itself."

"I already have one, though."

"Not like this, you don't."

I pull the jersey out of the box, the patches still stiff and new. Turning over the jersey to see the back, I freeze. Our names are on there together. Snow-Moxley, with his jersey number. The breath whooshes out of my lungs.

"El, it's—"

"It's a lot, I know, and I'm sorry. I just—God, I'm fucking this up—I always want you to be my Snow Queen, but I would love to see you with my name on your back too, like the other wives and girlfriends."

"You'd want me to?"

"I can't see anyone else wearing my jersey, having my name, or carrying my babies. You're it for me, and I'll wait for as long as it takes to make this happen, because I—I love you. If I need to go through another year as your go-to event face, or move mountains or—" I didn't let him finish his statement before I launch at him, kissing the breath out of his lungs. His arms instinctually wrapped around me at the same time as my ankles lock behind his back. "Is this a yes?"

"Yes yes yes, a thousand times, yes." I pepper kisses along his cheeks and neck, as he carries us across the hall. "Oh, Elliot, what were we thinking?"

"I'm going to go out on a limb and say that you were thinking this was against the rules, and I was too bullheaded to see what was right in front of me."

"That makes sense," I mutter against his lips, my hands tugging desperately against the t-shirt on his back, as his thread smoothly into my hair. "I'm so sorry I didn't see it before now, and why I let stupid La—" a large hand covered my mouth.

"No, don't say it. I don't want any of that getting in our way today. Just us, nothing else, no one else. No hockey, no publicity, or friends or anything."

"So does that mean you don't want to hear that I'm supposed to be back at the arena in an hour?"

He stops kissing my neck, before saying, "Call Jess and tell her you're tied up. You're not leaving here until at least tomorrow afternoon."

"But I'm not actually tied up," I argue.

"That could be arranged, if you ask nicely."

I pull my phone out of my pocket, hitting the dial button on Jess's number, before putting it on speaker phone.

"Hey Ronni! Are we still on for tonight?"

"No, I'm sorry, I'm going to need to cancel. Something's come up," I giggle as Elliot presses against me, "and I'm afraid I'm going to be tied up for a couple days." Elliot grins as he mouthed "good girl' to me.

"Oh, I get it," Jess chirps back. "Tell Elliot hey for me and you two kids have a grand time. Be safe! I'm glad you've made up!"

"Thanks, Jess," we both say at the same time before I hang up. "Oh my God, I can't believe we did that," I cackle as I throw my phone to the far side of the bed. "She's never going to let us live this down, you know."

"It's going to be fine. Now, where was I," he says before diving back down to plant kisses on my neck.

This wasn't totally the plan for the day, but it's far better than any previous plans I could have had.

CHAPTER 46

ELLIOT

IT HAS BEEN three weeks since Sami left for Vegas, and a week since she came home. She wouldn't tell me anything about how the trip went, if she had secured the marrow donation from her ex like she wanted. Hell, she hadn't said a single word about the whole trip, which was odd for her. I couldn't focus on that today, though, because I had something else more pressing to worry about at the moment.

I have every intention of proposing today during our friends and family skate before playoffs take us away. Bishop is in on it, naturally. Swear to God that man takes matchmaking to a whole new level. If he has any say in the matter, I'd think he would have had us married and moved in together weeks ago. I couldn't hate on him too hard about it though, because the man has the sound booth on speed dial for the Jumbotron slides.

Leaning against the boards by my home bench, my jersey-clad arms crossed across my chest, I watch on as Ronni plays with the kids at the far end of the rink. She surprised me this morning by walking out of her apartment–the one that sits empty more times than not–wearing *my* jersey. My number, my name spread out in large white letters across her back. I smirk as I think about it, and what happened when I pushed us back into her apartment. We almost didn't make it to the arena on time. Even now I can see my "68" peeking through her hair, and it makes me feral.

Words cannot describe what that vision does to me.

Sticking my hand in my pocket, I touch the soft velvet box tucked away in there. She saw the box when we reconciled before, but she never paid attention to what was in it. Sami knew, though. I glanced over to where Sami and Gabby were making their own circuit on the ice. Our grandmother's engagement ring was in my pocket. For the first time since we were kids, the ring would be on the hand of a Moxley woman again.

Bishop skates over to me, looking at the direction I stared in. "That woman really has you tied up in knots."

"Yep," I agree. "Wouldn't have it any other way, though."

"It's about that time. Are you ready?"

I suck in a sharp breath. "Yeah. Make the call."

Bishop pulls his phone from his back pocket and hammers out a quick text message, then puts his phone back as though nothing had happened. We watch and wait as the song blaring through the house speakers drew to a close, then the house lights dimmed, and small spotlights danced across the ice. On the large screens overhead, images of Ronni and me scrolled through with "Elliot loves Ronni" where our scores usually sit. The crowd grows silent around us, looking around to see what was going to happen next.

"Go get her, boy," Bishop grins as he punches me in the upper arm. I laugh and push off the boards, skating over toward Ronni who stood stock still, staring at me.

"Mox? What did you do, what's going on?"

I skate in a circle around her, running my fingers over the embroidered letters on her back, down her arm, to grasp her hand. I could feel the tremors, she's nervous. I jumped off script on her, and she doesn't know what to think of it. I skid to a halt in front of her, making her look up at me.

"Something," I answer, knowing she'd get riled at the non-answer.

"That isn't what I'm looking for and you know it."

"Hm, yeah, about that," I say thoughtfully, looking down at our joined hands. "I thought of something."

"Oh yeah? What's that?"

"I have an idea." I run my roughened fingertips over her soft knuckles, touching her left ring finger for a little longer than the others.

"What kind of idea is that?"

"I think you'll like it," I tease. "My idea is that we do something crazy this off-season." I swipe her knuckles again, trying not to get hypnotized by the way her hand felt in mine. "I want to move you into my apartment." I kiss her hand softly. "I want us to grow old together." Slowly, I drop to one knee on the ice, pulling the case out of my pocket. "I want to marry you, Ronni, if you'll have me. My Snow Queen, my love, will you marry me?"

She looks down at me, tears resting on her lashes. "Yes, yes, a million times over yes!" I brace myself to stand, only for Ronni to slip on her skates, knocking me backwards onto the ice. I wrap my arms around her, bracing her fall as she attacks my face with kisses. "You surprised me, I didn't know what was going on."

My empty hand roams into her hair. "I love you so much." I pull her head toward me, kissing her, reveling in the moment. Nothing exists outside her at the moment. "Come on, I'm not done yet." I gently move to sit up with her, opening the box and removing the golden band with the solitaire. "This was my grandmother's ring. My dad gave it to my mom, and she gave it to me to give to you." I slide it onto her finger, ecstatic that it fit perfectly. "We can add to it if you want, so it's unique to you, or even pick your own—"

"No, I love it just the way it is." She held out her shaky hand to admire the lights in the arena glinting off of it. "Oh, Elliot, I love you." Her hands came up to rest alongside my cheeks, before her lips pressed to mine. "I love you, I love you, I love you."

Gradually, I notice the surrounding applause, and with a cracked eye take in the crowd of friends and family around us. "I think we may need to say something soon," I whisper to her, stealing another kiss along her jaw.

Carefully, she gets back on her skates, and I stand beside her. She looks up into my eyes, and we both grin.

"We're getting married!" We both yell simultaneously, before Bishop, Jess, and Sami launched at us.

"I'm getting an aunt! That's freaking awesome! Congratulations, Uncle El! Can I call you Aunt Ronni?"

Gabby's small arms wrap around both of us, and I gather her up before she gets lost in the scrum.

"Absolutely, Gabby! I'd love that!" Ronni leans in to me and wraps her arm around Gabby's back.

"It's about damn time you got your head on straight, El! Welcome to the family, Ronni!"

"Hell yeah, Mox, you did it! Congrats you two," Bishop says, dropping a firm clap to my back.

The congratulations continue to come until I eventually pull Ronni away from the crowd, and to the bench.

"Jess, you have control of this event, right? I want to take my fiancée home," I call out to her.

"You know it. Go celebrate together! Have fun!"

We say our goodbyes, with Ronni giving Jess a hug. Grasping Ronni's hand, we run down the tunnel toward the locker room.

"Hold on, hotshot." She pulls back on my hand, slowing me down. I look down at our joined hands and back at her, eyebrows furrowed. "Come here." She pushes open the doorway for the training room, the room I pulled her in months ago to steal pre-game kisses. Without turning on the lights, she shuts the door, locking us inside.

"This is where it all started," I say into the dark, reaching out for her. She willingly slips into my hold, wrapping her arms up and around my neck as I dip my head down toward hers. Her lips meet mine in a feverish kiss, her moan vibrating against my chest.

Her fingers slide into my hair, her nails grazing my scalp sending tingles down my spine.

"I cut you short, and you wore my lipstick out on the ice," she whispers against my jaw, trailing kisses down my neck.

"You did," I agree as my hands slid down to her thighs, hoisting her up to wrap her legs around my hips. "But there's not a game today, so we have nothing but time now." Two steps forward, and I sit her on the table. My hands slide up and under the hem of the jersey. "Have I told you how fucking hot you are with my name and number on your back?" I growl, kissing her hard. "It took all I had not to come after you earlier."

"You should have, we could have done this earlier." She moans, grabbing my collar to pull me toward her again. "And again now. And then when we get back to our house."

I groan and pull back from her, looking her square in the face. "I really like the way this sounds," I whisper, trailing my fingers around her waistband, "our house. God, I want you to move in right now."

"In a minute. I want something else now." Her legs tighten around me, pulling me toward her. "Please, El."

"Listen to you, begging," I grit out as she rolls her hips against me. "Can you stay quiet for me, baby? We don't want anyone to hear."

"I'll be quiet, I swear."

"Good girl," I whisper against her ear as I unfasten her

jeans. "Hop down, turn around." She followed my instructions, pressing her forearms down on the table as I slide her jeans down, pushing her jersey up the slightest bit, smoothing my hands along her exposed lower back and across the curve of her hip. "Gorgeous. Stay put, and remember to be quiet." She nods her head, and I bite my lip as I unfasten my own jeans, edging close enough to her I could feel her thighs trembling against my own. I slipped my length along her crease, just enough to tease the both of us. She bites back a whimper as I slide fully into her, and I grit my teeth at the same time.

"Oh God, El," she whispers, rocking back against me. "I love you, I love you, oh please please please-" she moans as I pull out and ease back in, my hands grabbing her hips as I grind back into her.

"That's my girl," I praise, thrusting faster, "look at you, taking it so well." I revel in the feel of her around me, her soft sounds, and double my efforts. Her quiet whimpers grow louder, but I can tell she's trying to keep her noises muffled. "Shh, you don't want anyone to know we're in here."

"Trying, it's just so good, I—" She cuts off with her hand over her own mouth, and I grind deeper against her, feeling her flutter against me.

"Yes, just like that," I groan back, feeling like I'm going to follow her over that cliff. My heart races, and I grunt, dropping my head against her shoulder. As my breathing and pulse slow to its normal rhythm, I kiss the back of her neck. Wrapping my arms around her, I feel her own pulse against my hand. "God, I love you."

"Same," she whispers, resting her head against her forearms. "Can we go home now? I have plans for you."

"In a minute," I murmur against her neck, before pushing myself back upright and fixing our clothing.

"Let's go home," she whispers, popping up on her toes to kiss me.

"Absolutely. I can't wait."

I peek out the door to make sure the door was clear, before ushering her out into the hall and making our way to the parking lot. Her hand slides comfortably into mine, and I can't stop myself from lifting that hand with my ring glittering on it to my lips.

From here on out, I swore to myself, we would be making this path together, every day. My Snow Queen.

THE END

ACKNOWLEDGMENTS

I started writing out "thank you" notes in my dedication and realized that giving everyone who played a part in this ample thanks was going to be a whole book by itself.

First and foremost, I need to thank my husband. My tattooed badass. The poor dude that has to listen to me ramble about imaginary people in my head and then tell him he'll be eye candy at my book signings. I'm so grateful that you put up with my shit. :) Same for the kids, who have been under advisement to only disrupt me if someone is bleeding or the house is on fire before. I love you all so much.

Rose, Rose, Rose…you're the all-star MVP! I can't give you enough thanks for my cover art and formatting. You rock, and Tripping wouldn't be what it is without you! I promise to lay off the tab button the next time. :)

Sheri: Thank you so much for proofreading, and not letting me settle for a couple "fade to black" scenes or skipping the details!

Paige, my alpha baby. You put up with my "here's a chapter! Here's another chapter! Here's another one!" Also, the double spaces after periods in the early days. You're freaking awesome, and I love your face!

The Romance Riot. This amazing group of chaos goblins have been a force of nature, and I don't know where I would have been without them. Need cheerleaders? They're there. Need betas or tech support? Got it. I can't believe how quickly y'all have become a part of my writing journey, and that you've let me tag along on your own as well.

As I move forward with The Sin Bin Series, I hope that everyone loves the little group of friends and family that I've created in the Ice Wolves universe. I've loved building this little team and look forward to releasing them into the universe for you all.

ABOUT THE AUTHOR

Eden Knox is a sports romance author who lives in Ohio with her 2 girls, herd of animals, and her "looks like could kill you, is a cinnamon roll" husband. When she isn't screaming at hockey or football games, she's working on tormenting her fictional hockey team or completing coursework for grad school. Currently, she is working on book 3 in The Sin Bin Series, Hooking Up With Number 36.

instagram.com/edenknoxwrites
facebook.com/eden.knox.145432
tiktok.com/@edenknoxwrites

ALSO BY EDEN KNOX

Fighting for Number 57

Hooking Up With Number 36

On the Breakaway: Short Stories From The Sin Bin